W.CRISP

GW00775837

AK
I.McD

KINGFISHER DAYS

Antonia Everett-Cox is extremely worried when her half-brother, Maximilian, fails to make an appearance at her birthday party. He had been exploring the jungles of the Caribbean, but he should have returned to London by now. Antonia decides she must go and search for Max. She had always been a sophisticated city girl, but when she hires Jack Bentley's sailing boat in the Caribbean she is thrown into an alien world of adventure, danger — and romance, against all the odds!

Books by Louise Armstrong
in the Linford Romance Library:

LOUISE ARMSTRONG

◆

KINGFISHER DAYS

Complete and Unabridged

LINFORD
Leicester

First published in Great Britain in 2001

First Linford Edition
published 2002

British Library CIP Data

Armstrong, Louise
    Kingfisher days.—Large print ed.—
Linford romance library
1. Love stories
2. Large type books
I. Title
823.9'14 [F]

ISBN 0–7089–9892–5

Published by
F. A. Thorpe (Publishing)
Anstey, Leicestershire
Set by Words & Graphics Ltd.
Anstey, Leicestershire
Printed and bound in Great Britain by
T. J. International Ltd., Padstow, Cornwall

This book is printed on acid-free paper

1

Antonia Everett-Cox pushed in front of the hired maid to answer the door herself. Disappointment bruised her heart when she saw that it wasn't the guest she'd been waiting for.

'Antonia, sweetie! Happy birthday,' the rake-thin fashion model who was standing there said.

'Thank you, darling,' Antonia replied, kissing the air on each side of her friend's cheek. 'So nice of you to come.'

As she entered Antonia's Kensington home, the model forgot her carefully-cultivated sophistication and stared openly at the newly-done Fifties'-style decor. Her tone expressed complete disbelief.

'My dear! Did you steal that carpet from the pub down the road?'

'Orange and yellow swirls are so fashionable now,' Antonia told her firmly, although privately she wasn't at all sure about them herself. 'Come and put a coin in the jukebox. It's the most fun.'

Then Antonia waved at one of the uniformed maids and took a glass of bubbly off the silver tray she was holding.

'Try one of these,' she told her friend, and escaped into the drawing-room with a whirl of her Fifties' skirt.

Another disappointment, she thought. She'd have to stop hoping that every knock on the door would be a message from her half-brother. She didn't really expect Maximilian himself, of course. He was roaming around in some ghastly bit of jungle in the Caribbean somewhere, but if he couldn't come himself, he always sent a message or a present, usually both.

It was a long-standing tradition between them and he'd never failed. Antonia looked at her watch and bit her lip. There were only ten minutes left to midnight. He would have to get a move on if he was going to make it.

'Antonia!'

Her favourite man in the whole world moved towards her with a smile in his grey eyes.

'A triumph as usual.'

There was a stability and niceness about Hugh that drew her like a bee to honey.

'Give me a birthday kiss,' she begged.

His grey eyes were grave and steady.

'Fiona sends her love, and so do Pippin and Elf. Enjoy the rest of your holiday.'

She caught his hands.

'Hugh! You're not leaving.'

'I've an early round tomorrow.'

Antonia flipped a tress of long, highlighted dark hair forwards and peeped through it flirtatiously.

'I'm sick! I'm very, very sick. I need you more than your patients do.'

His grey eyes regarded her quizzically.

'I've never thought of you as needing anything or anyone. You're the original golden girl, Antonia.'

'Well, you're wrong,' she told him. 'I'm worried sick about Max.'

Hugh suddenly looked every inch the reassuring doctor.

'I joined in this conversation earlier. How long did the list of reasons get?'

'Oh, I think there were eighty-nine good reasons why a man couldn't send a birthday card from a remote Caribbean island on time. But you don't understand. Max has never, ever failed before, and it's at least three months since anyone heard from him.'

'Your brother can look after himself, Antonia,' a dreamy voice said from behind them.

She whirled impatiently.

'But, Daddy, what if he's sick in the jungle?'

Her father waved a gently-dismissive hand.

'He'll come back when he's ready.'

The Fifties' clock on the mantelpiece struck twelve silvery notes. Antonia was shaken by a wave of real fear and apprehension that settled in her stomach like a stone. She'd been expecting a last-minute diversion, she realised. A kiss-o-gram perhaps, or an orang-utan at the doorway bearing a joking message from her brother. The bond between her half-brother and herself was a real one, and it had never been broken before.

'Max must be in trouble,' she announced.

Her father didn't even look at her.

'I doubt it,' he replied. 'Hugh, if you're leaving, shall we share a taxi?'

Antonia felt a rush of anger.

'You're not taking this seriously,' she exclaimed. 'If you won't do anything about it, I shall go and look for him myself!'

'Just as you like, my dear,' her father said, leaving the room with Hugh.

Antonia stared at his departing back in fury. The very real fear for her brother that washed around her system wouldn't let her rest. She ran out into the hall after the two men. Hugh and her father were waiting for their coats. They didn't see her.

'What a child Antonia is,' her father sighed. 'Max doesn't come to her party, so she thinks he's on the brink of death. I hope she doesn't go rushing abroad after him.'

'Not likely,' Hugh said, smiling a thank-you at the maid and taking his coat from her. 'I just don't see her as the type to take the initiative and do something that positive and daring.'

The manservant opened the door. Antonia started shivering as a gust of cold air blew into the hall. Her father turned to Hugh as if he was agreeing with him.

'No moral fibre, I'm afraid. She never had any backbone.'

The door was closed and Antonia stood, trembling all over. She'd never seen much of her father, but she'd always vaguely assumed that he liked and approved of her. Fathers had to approve of their daughters, didn't they? And Hugh! When she was six years old, she had told Hugh that she wanted to marry him and she'd never changed her mind since.

Unfortunately, he'd remained oblivious to her advances, but he was still the one man in London whose opinion she respected, whose goodwill she sought, and to hear him dismiss her so casually was a pain that cut deep. She felt betrayed, dismissed, as if she and her opinions meant nothing. Surely she knew more about the bond between herself and her half-brother than anyone else? Yet they'd brushed aside her fears as if they were trivial.

The front door bell rang. She tensed hopefully, but it was more guests arriving. Antonia whirled on her heel and ran upstairs. Her bedroom was full of coats, and people were in and out, so it offered no refuge. She sat at her dressing-table and picked up a brush. Her normally cover-girl perfection was shattered. She'd repair the damage and go back to her party. Her eyes still showed the pain of overhearing her father and Hugh, and the very real fear that had lurked all day and grown monstrously since midnight.

As an anthropologist with his own funds, Max, the son of her father's second wife, frequently spent months in remote areas. But no matter where he went, even if he had to enrol a friend and make his arrangements months ahead, he never, ever forgot her birthday.

She stared at her reflection in the mirror and watched the pupils of her eyes dilate. Hugh and her father could say what they liked. She knew her brother. If he hadn't contacted her today, it was because he couldn't. And I've got enough brains to see that something needs doing about it, Antonia told herself, before slipping downstairs to suffer the rest of her party.

2

Antonia followed the small boy who'd met the ship and appointed himself her guide. He led her on to a rickety jetty that ran over sea water as green as an opal and then on to the hot white sand of the beach. Antonia came to a dead halt and her brow puckered in a frown.

'What do you mean, there are no taxis?'

Her diminutive escort flashed her the brightest of smiles.

'You walk to hotel, Miss Antonia. It not far.'

Antonia pulled down her sunglasses and examined his face carefully. He didn't look as if he were joking. It was boiling hot on the beach. Antonia realised she'd better get moving. She waded through the soft sand and on to a dirt path that wound towards a grove of palm trees.

'This way?' she asked the young boy who was guiding her.

His face split in a blissful smile.

'Best hotel in town, miss, and when you want a boat, you ask for Jack.'

He set off down the path, cheerfully hefting one of Antonia's suitcases under each arm. Her matching handbag, camera, day pack and beach bag were hung around his neck. She followed him. The strong, sweet smell of copra hung in the air, and the humidity was so thick that walking through the air was like pushing through a soft, damp curtain.

Three weeks ago, I couldn't have done this, she thought. She couldn't help being pleased at the thought Hugh and her father could lump it.

She had to admit that the first part of her trip had been easy. The Caribbean was hardly off the beaten track. All she'd had to do was wave her credit card at the airline and be wafted away to paradise. After that, the going had become steadily harder. She might well have given up, except for the fact that no-one had heard from Max since he'd flown to Jamaica and made a base camp there.

Antonia had gone straight to the hotel Max had given as a forwarding address. His mail was piling up behind the desk and the clerk didn't seem at all interested in the fact that he hadn't turned up to collect it. Neither, when she eventually tracked him down, did the manager. The island police shrugged their shoulders. The coast-guard said that it was nothing to do with them. When she finally got an appointment with a British consul, he wasn't any help either.

'Why is it,' Antonia asked, 'that I am the only person on the whole planet who is worried about the fact that my brother is missing?'

The consul shrugged and looked bored.

'He isn't missing, officially.'

Antonia gritted her teeth.

'I know he didn't lodge a return date

11

with you, but I've explained how he never misses my birthday.'

'Why don't you ask around?' he suggested. 'If you could come up with proof he was in trouble I might be able to do something, but as it is, young men in the tropics often switch to island time and forget to write home. The relatives turn up here panicking, but believe me, my dear, nine times out of ten the disappearance has been caused by nothing more sinister than sunshine and island rum.'

He stood up, but Antonia ignored the signal to leave.

'But Max didn't come here to bum around the beaches. He's a working anthropologist.'

Unmoved, the consul opened the door. There was no point in antagonising the man. Antonia stood up and gave him her best smile.

'Thank you so much for your help,' she told him. 'I'll take your advice, and may I come back to you if I need any more help?'

The consul softened visibly as he met the full force of her smile.

'Anything I can do,' he promised, with more goodwill than accuracy.

Antonia then stood in the hot, busy street, clutching her bag and trying to calm the frantic butterflies in her stomach. She felt very alone. Whatever officialdom said, her intuition told her that Max was missing. She reached deep into a place in her mind she'd never explored before and found strength. Clearly, her brother had to be found, and equally clearly, she was the one who'd have to do it.

And so, feeling like a detective, she'd followed the trail. It was easy enough to find out which boat he'd taken. The woman in the harbour office remembered him because, typical Max, he'd chatted her up while he was buying his ticket! Antonia had taken the daily steamer to one island, hung around for the weekly boat to an even smaller one, and there, by a great stroke of good fortune, connected with one of the itinerant tramp boats that puffed their way around the islands, stopping wherever there was a fare to be made. This took her on to Swimp Island.

And now, here she was, approaching the only hotel on an island so small it appeared like a fly speck on the largest scale map she'd been able to buy. The hotel owner seemed very surprised to see her. He flicked a grubby cloth across his bar and looked puzzled.

'What you want with Jack Bentley? He owe you money?'

'No.'

A drop of sweat dribbled down Antonia's back. The only fan on the ceiling moved so slowly that flies clung to the broad blades and buzzed around it in clouds. Reggae music played softly from a dark corner of the bar, but the only other customer, an old man, was sound asleep.

The barman had been thinking things over. His black eyes roamed over Antonia's elegant dress and slightly tanned limbs. She plonked her make-up

14

case on the bar and stared directly into the man's suspicious eyes.

'Can I book a room?'

The resulting bedroom was a disaster. Dust lay thick on the bamboo furniture and cobwebs lurked in the grimy corners.

'Is there a room maid?' Antonia asked, flicking a finger over one of the many cigarette burns that disfigured the furniture.

'She might be sleeping.'

Antonia stripped the grubby sheets off the bed and pushed them into the arms of the hotel keeper.

'Have her wash those, please, and I'd like someone to put my mattress in the sun for at least four hours, turning it every hour.'

The man blinked at her in a dozy manner over his armful of laundry.

★ ★ ★

Jack Bentley leaned against the corrugated iron walls of the island's only shop and squinted at the light of the bar entrance across the dusty street. He was a moderate man when it came to alcohol, and he knew when he'd had enough, but he'd made the mistake of matching the hollow-legged Curly down at Lena's shack on the harbour. It had been a mistake, but it had been so good to get back on shore, so incredibly good to get rid of the loud, bulky, obnoxious, rich businessmen who'd chartered his boat and made him and Curly so miserable over the last week.

Jack grinned again. They'd done well. They'd stuck it out. They'd found fish, hadn't punched one single passenger and the customers had gone home happy. He and Curly had stood on the deck of his boat, the Kingfisher, doing a war dance as the hired helicopter disappeared over the horizon, carrying the businessmen away for good. Then they'd gone to Lena's, and now all he had to do was get home.

For some reason it seemed important to climb very, very quietly up the sagging iron fire-escape that ran up to the balcony where the bedrooms were. Once up on the balcony Jack dug in the pocket of his tattered denim shorts for his keys. He clutched an iron strut for support and counted the row of doors.

'One, two, buckle my shoe. I guess that one's mine.'

The key spun in the lock but didn't catch properly. Jack paused, wiped his brow and looked down his nose in a determined squint.

'Come on, you little beauty, open for Uncle Jack.'

He nodded in satisfaction as the lock clicked open. He tottered into the room and stood inside swaying slightly. It smelled unfamiliar but gorgeous. The air was heavy with perfume.

'Gee, who's sent me flowers?' he muttered, pushing his heavy dark fringe off his forehead, blinking at a bunch of tropical blooms on top of the bedside table.

They glowed in the moonlight that filtered into the room. Then Jack looked at the bed. Lying under the whitest sheet he'd ever seen, with her dark curls tumbled over a milk-white pillow, looking just like a fairy-tale illustration, lay Snow White! After a moment's astonishment, Jack's mouth stretched wide in a smile as he made to close the door, which creaked loudly. The dark head stirred on the pillows. She sat up, clutching the sheet around her. Jack peered more closely.

'I can't remember you, but,' he said confidentially with a grin, 'I've been drinking, you see.'

'I certainly do see,' she said icily. 'What are you doing in my room?'

Jack blinked.

'Could we have arranged to meet earlier?'

Through his sleepy haze Jack saw her get up from the bed, wrapping the sheet around her slender body. Was it his eyes, or was she bending over the bedside table? He felt confused.

'Room's spinning,' he said weakly.

Jack heard the rasp of a match, and

then the female straightened up, looking like a Greek goddess draped as she was in yards of white cotton. She lifted the polished tin lamp she had just lit. The soft glow of the lamplight fell over her face, neck and shoulders, and Jack felt as if he'd never truly seen a woman before.

He looked into the sapphire chips of her eyes and was lost. The dark mass of her hair tumbled silkily over her tanned shoulders. Brown eyebrows arched in a pure line over almond-shaped eyelids starred by silky black lashes. His gaze fell on a pink leaf of a mouth.

Tipsy or not, there was only one thing for a man to do. He reached for her with both arms and bent his head towards her. Antonia froze as the man's mouth touched hers lightly. His touch sent her limp and dizzy. She took a step backwards and fell over backwards on to the bed. Common-sense returned with a snap. She twisted her head away from his lips and lifted her hands and pushed against the muscles of his chest.

The stranger merely laughed out loud. She lay, looking up at the strong planes of his face in the lamplight. Dark hair fell forward over his forehead and curled thickly at the back of his neck.

'You're some high-class woman, you are,' he said softly, admiringly.

Antonia held very still until his lips touched hers once again. Then she sank her teeth into his tender under-lip. He exhaled sharply and sat back on his knees, raising one hand to touch the injured lip.

Antonia grabbed hold of one of his knees and lifted and twisted at the same time, hoping to unbalance him. Once she'd got him moving, the man's weight and size helped carry him over the edge of the bed and on to the bare boards of the floor with a heavy and satisfying thump.

Pulling up her slipping sheet, Antonia lunged across the room and grabbed at the sweeping brush she'd been using earlier. She got her back to the wall by the head of the bed and stared at the man on the floor.

'So lucky no-one wanted this brush back,' she told him. 'I feel so much better with a weapon in my hands.'

He was still sitting on the floor, holding his head in his hands.

'Take it easy, lady,' he begged, lifting his head slightly and regarding her with a wary look in his eyes.

She could hear his Australian accent now. It didn't make her feel any better. She lifted her chin and spoke icily.

'I don't see how I can relax with a strange man in my room, not knowing what he's up to.'

The man blinked at her.

'You think I'm going to hurt you?'

'You stopped by my room in the middle of the night for an innocent chat, did you?'

'Been a mistake,' he said.

He fumbled in his pocket. Metal clinked as he pulled out a bunch of keys. He found the room key and held it out triumphantly to Antonia.

'You're in my room.'

Curious, she took the key from him. It was the key for room six.

'This is room nine,' she told him. 'You are in my room.'

Now that she knew the intruder was a fellow guest, Antonia felt fear and tension drain out of her.

She gestured at the door with the brush.

'If you wouldn't mind going.'

The man got clumsily to his feet and stood there swaying slightly.

'I wouldn't mind going at all now I recognise your accent,' he told her. 'I hate you stuck-up Brits.'

'Well, go find yourself a drunken Australian!' Antonia exploded.

Dark eyes flashed in the lamplight.

'That's right, look down your nose at a fella, just because he's had a drink or two. If only you knew what I'd taken from those yucky-yucky rich creeps who chartered my boat this week, you'd give me a medal, never mind a beer or two. I took it from them because I had to, but I don't have to take it from you, lady, so don't push me around.'

Antonia lowered the broom handle.

'Wait a minute. Did you say you chartered a boat?'

The man finally got one hand on the door handle and managed to turn it, but he stopped with the door open a crack.

'Only when I have to.'

Antonia turned the lamp up full and hung it on the hook in the centre of the room.

'Then you must be Jack Bentley.'

He turned around and looked at her. She could see now that his eyes were a deep brown hazel colour and they seemed to be sobering rapidly. His chin looked strong and stubborn under the dark stubble.

'Wait a moment,' Antonia said.

She checked that the sheet was still securely wrapped around her body.

'Maybe we should start over. I'm here to charter your boat.'

His eyes narrowed slightly and he laughed to himself.

23

'Don't have to charter the Kingfisher until next year now, maybe not even then if my invest — .'

He broke off.

'Never mind about that. Those disgusting men paid me a fat, city fortune. I'm a free man now.'

It was not the answer Antonia had been expecting. Her eyes flew open in astonishment.

'Everyone said you'd take me.'

'Should have thought of that before you hit me with the broom,' he told her, and he turned towards the door again.

Antonia found the impulse to argue was strong, but what was more important — proving she was in the right, or finding Max?

'I'm sorry we got off to a bad start,' she said truthfully. 'I'm sure if I explain about my brother you'll want to help me.'

Jack had opened the door fully, but he turned slightly to look at her. Light from the lamp illuminated his stern features. Antonia met his hard eyes with a shock.

He doesn't even know me, she thought, but the look in his eyes says that he's judged me and found me wanting. It was no surprise to hear the cold note in his vice.

'I know all about it, mate. You and your mad crusade is the talk of the island. Your brother's probably enjoying some freedom. You should go back to your family fortune and leave him to it.'

'No!'

'Suit yourself, lady, but I'm not interested.'

He squared his shoulders and marched out of Antonia's room. Only a slight stumble as his bare foot hit an uneven board on the balcony spoiled the outraged dignity of his departure. Antonia re-locked her door and wedged the broom handle across it for good measure.

'Ha!' she muttered to herself as she remade the bed and got into it. 'So Mr Jack Bentley doesn't believe in equality for the rich?'

She thumped the pillow.

'I don't need that creep. I'll find someone else to rent me a boat.'

And with that comforting thought, she composed herself for sleep.

3

The next morning, Jack sat with his bare feet wedged on the balcony rail of the hotel veranda, nursing his hangover. He tipped his hat farther over his eyes and wished he hadn't left his sunglasses on board the Kingfisher. The light was just too bright today.

A swirl of bougainvillaea pink caught his attention as Antonia came into sight at the bottom of the dusty street, followed by her devoted guide, little Buddy. She was walking up the left-hand side of the road, knocking on the door of each shack she came to. She was obviously determined to ask every single person on the island about transport to Sugar Cay, Jack thought, watching her vanish inside a small hovel.

She wouldn't be in there long. She wouldn't find anyone who could take her. The islanders only went to sea to catch fish, using shallow-bottomed, tin boats that wouldn't stand up to the heavy seas outside the reef. If they wanted to go anywhere else they waited for a steamer.

Antonia and Buddy emerged from the shack and went on to knock at the door of the next one. Jack studied her carefully. Her tip-tilted chin held a determination that was at odds with her fashion-plate figure. This time she wasn't invited inside. She looked like an angel as she stood in the hot street, explaining her mission, but the figure who had answered her knock was shaking his head firmly. Undeterred, Antonia went on to the next house.

'Do you good to learn money can't buy everything, lady,' Jack said softly to himself.

Yet he was surprised to find himself feeling sorry for her. Island gossip had it that she'd been up since dawn, and if she'd already been down the right-hand side of the street, then she had spoken to every single person on Swimp Island. She was no quitter, that was for sure.

But she's rich, and that means trouble, he reminded himself. Your policy is to stay out of trouble. He closed his eyes and tried to sleep off his headache, but a few minutes later he sensed Antonia approaching. As soon as he heard her soft footsteps and smelled her floral perfume, he knew that he'd really been waiting to talk to her again.

'Twelve o'clock and you've done the island,' he remarked coolly, glancing at his watch. 'You ready to go home now?'

When he looked at her, he saw that his tone had hurt her. Her eyes were so sad that he couldn't meet them. His gaze moved over her face. A light dew of sweat gleamed on her perfect skin, and he saw her throat move convulsively. The pink lips quivered.

'You're the only person who can help me. Please, will you take me to Sugar Cay to look for my brother?'

Jack's heart twisted. She was so alone. Was he feeling sorry for the enemy? Maybe a little, he acknowledged, as he looked at her. If you pencilled on whiskers, she'd look just like a lost kitten. He'd have to be made of stone not to look into those vulnerable eyes and not want to help her. He supposed he could.

'I'd pay you double,' Antonia was saying.

Jack couldn't believe how close he'd come to falling for the act.

'It always comes back to money with your type,' he snapped at her.

She looked baffled by his vehemence.

'I didn't mean to insult you.'

He closed his eyes, sure now that he'd made the right decision.

'No.'

'Please?' she said softly.

Jack ignored the pleading note in her voice and focused on how much he hated upper-class accents.

'Unlike Buddy, not everyone on this island is for sale.'

Buddy's voice piped up indignantly.

'You're in some bad mood, Jack!

Miss Antonia's cool!'

At the same moment Antonia cried, 'Buddy gives all his wages to his mother! Pick on someone your own age and weight, you total blob!'

'Blob?' Jack roared, opening his eyes wide.

He felt pretty mean inside. Antonia's gaze was scathing.

'Blob,' she repeated firmly. 'A scruffy, unshaven, hung-over blob.'

She turned to her adoring guide.

'Buddy, it's time you and I had a long, cool drink in some pleasant company.'

In a whirl of sweet scent, she marched straight past Jack, leaving him feeling that he hadn't shown up very well in the encounter. But he still wasn't going to take her to Sugar Cay. He'd made his mind up about that.

Much later that night, Antonia woke up in the hot, humid darkness and opened her mouth to scream. A hand covered her mouth. After a few heart-thumping seconds she recognised the body that hovered over hers.

'Jack?'

'Don't scream,' he warned her, and took his hand away.

Antonia became aware of heavy footsteps rocking the room as what sounded like a posse of men charged to the end of the balcony outside.

'Hiding from your fan club?' she enquired tartly.

She saw his white teeth flash in the dim silver moonlight.

'I can explain.'

She was suddenly angry. She pushed at his rock-solid body and managed to drag herself against the pillows.

'Why should I hide you?'

As fast as a snake striking, his hand went back over her mouth. She saw a flash of anger in his dark eyes.

'Keep your voice down.'

She glared right back, feeling pretty angry herself. She owed Jack Bentley less than nothing, except maybe a lesson. He had no right to invade her privacy this way. Her body stiffened. As soon as he took his hand away, she was going to scream. His dark eyes scanned her face as if he was reading her mind.

'Do you still want to charter the Kingfisher?'

Outside, an angry voice roared.

'Jack! We're going to get you!'

Antonia cocked her head to one side and regarded the man seated on her bed.

'You and your boat are suddenly free to travel, is that it?'

'How does five thousand US dollars sound?'

'Way over the top,' Antonia said, comfortably aware that she had the upper hand as long as the search party was thumping around outside.

She boxed clever.

'Three thousand? Half now, half when we get back.'

'It's a deal,' Jack said, grinning.

He sat on the side of the bed and ran his fingers through his thick dark hair. The balcony rattled as what sounded like a dozen heavy men thumped down the fire escape.

'It might be difficult to pay you local currency,' Antonia said, frowning. 'How do people live without cash machines?'

'I'll take travellers' cheques,' Jack offered cheerfully.

Antonia took her handbag from under her pillow. She took out a book of cheques and counted out fifteen hundred dollars.

'I'll leave the other half behind the bar,' she told him, 'along with a letter telling the British Consul where I'm going.'

'You trust the bartender more than me?'

She frowned. Then she had a totally brilliant idea.

'I'll leave it with Buddy and his mother,' she said. 'I trust them.'

'Suit yourself,' Jack replied, holding out his hand.

Antonia paused in the act of handing over the money. The instinct that had made her take precautions was still not satisfied. Was Jack on the level? Her eyes searched his face.

'What time shall we leave?'

Jack's grin was too bland, too accommodating.

'How does nine o'clock tomorrow sound?' he asked.

'Perfectly lovely,' Antonia murmured.

Her feeling of unease increased as Jack swung off the bed, pocketed the cheques and slipped away with a cheery wave, checking the surroundings carefully before he actually went through the door.

Antonia sat bolt upright in the empty room. She put her hands to her stomach.

'Butterflies,' she murmured, 'I know something's wrong.'

After a moment's further thought she slipped on a cotton dress, silently left the room and headed for Buddy's house.

★ ★ ★

Jack felt a moment's regret as he opened the door of Lena's shack.

'I hate to disturb you, Curly, old mate,' he murmured softly.

Curly blinked sleepily at his friend.

'This had better be good.'

Jack chuckled softly.

'Stay if you want.'

Curly yawned.

'You shipping out?'

'As of now. I got a few sacks of noodles here. Get Lena to row you out in her dinghy, will you? I want to use the boat's dinghy to fill up with the rest of the provisions.'

Jack saw the flash of white teeth as Curly yawned again, but he shuffled over to the fire.

'You murder someone?' he asked, stirring the embers, and shaking the kettle to see if there was any hot water.

'I got lucky in business,' Jack told him with a straight face.

Lena had evidently been listening.

'If you boys so lucky, what's with the midnight flit?' she demanded.

'It's more exciting,' Jack told her.

Lena grumbled at him, but as she came closer, Jack saw that she was grinning, so he knew that she'd row Curly out to the Kingfisher. Smiling softly, he slipped back out into the darkness.

It took him longer than he'd expected to round up all the provisions and get his dinghy going, but that was partly because he'd had to make a wide detour after nearly getting caught at the store. He'd given them the slip, though. He laughed to himself at the memory, and then he slapped his thigh in annoyance. In all the fuss he'd forgotten to leave Antonia's travellers' cheques at Buddy's place.

Jack looked back over his shoulder at the dark shape of the jetty. Tall figures stood on the end of it, waving and gesticulating towards him. No way he could go back now the search party had discovered him. He shrugged philosophically and looked back out to sea. He'd shred the cheques in the morning.

Antonia could report them stolen and get replacements. She didn't look like a few days without money would hurt her.

She's a rich woman, he reminded himself as his little dinghy purred across the moon-silvered water to where the white shape of the Kingfisher swung at anchor under the stars. You don't need to feel bad if she thinks you tricked her out of a few dollars.

But he did.

There was no sign of another dinghy as he came up to his boat and tied up, but a faint glow coming through the portholes told of light in the cabin below. Lena must have dropped Curly and gone back to shore. Jack supposed it was a bit mean to drag Curly away from Lena, but he knew his friend wouldn't dream of staying behind if the Kingfisher was leaving.

Jack sometimes wondered if sailing would be so much fun without Curly, but there was no need to worry. After nearly three years, their friendship was stronger than ever. Jack hoisted the first sack of supplies on his shoulder and climbed the chrome ladder that hung over the low transom of the boat.

'Curly?' he called.

There was no answer, and a flicker of unease ran up his spine. Jack put the sack down and held his breath as he listened. Nothing stirred but a faint sea-breeze that lifted a few strands of his hair. It wasn't like Curly to go to sleep with adventure afoot. Jack felt so uncomfortable that he looked around him for a weapon, finally selecting a heavy winch handle. He tiptoed down the wooden ladder that led into the cabin. He froze at the foot of the ladder and his jaw dropped open in astonishment.

Sitting primly at the cabin table was Antonia. She looked more than ever like a debutante, or a magazine model advertising expensive watches. Her make-up case was plonked on the table in front of her, and her other luggage made a vast heap on the bench seat that ran around the table. His concentration flickered for a second. How could such a tiny woman need such huge suitcases? Then he got serious.

'Where's Curly?' he snapped.

Antonia looked at him sweetly as she replied, 'Locked in the lavatory.'

Jack lifted the winch handle and took a step forward.

'What's he doing?'

And then he saw that she was holding a gun, pointed at him. Antonia held the gun steady and smiled again. She raised her voice.

'He's perfectly happy in there, aren't you, Curly?'

Jack could hear the laughter in the muffled voice that came through the wood of the door.

'Best place to be in the circumstances.'

In spite of himself, Jack started to smile.

'I didn't know you two knew each other.'

Antonia waved the gun airily.

'We're totally on the same wave-length,' she told Jack gravely. 'Like you, he thinks that we should leave now and avoid the traffic.'

Jack stared at her deceptive, kitten-like sweetness and felt nothing but admiration. She was groomed down to her last dark hair and her eyes sparkled with fun. She was enjoying herself! Jack admired her even more.

'You win and congratulations on getting here under your own steam!'

Antonia studied his face for a moment and then put the gun away. Jack opened the door to the ship's toilet, and Curly appeared, looking cheerful. Despite his deep, gravely voice, he produced a remarkably convincing society tone.

'Jack, darling! How often have we said to each other that we simply have to make the time to visit the Sugar Cay islands?'

Jack started to grin and then broke out into a rolling chuckle.

'My dear Curly,' he simpered, 'it must be every day.'

'I can't wait to set sail!'

Jack laughed again.

'Then let's get up the anchor!'

42

4

Antonia felt pure satisfaction as Curly and Jack pulled on various ropes and winches. The boat's white sails flapped noisily in the darkness and the anchor chain rattled as it was drawn on board.

The Kingfisher turned her nose and Antonia felt a shiver run through the boat as she crested the first wave of the journey. The sails flapped again, and then turned into full-bellied wings as the wind caught them. The boat leaped ahead faster.

'This is exciting!' she cried jubilantly.

Jack set the boat on a course out to sea, and then gave the wheel to Curly and came over to the rail, where Antonia was standing, too excited to sit down.

'It'll take us several days to get to the next island, Galliwasp,' he explained.

'I'll go over the route with you tomorrow, if you like, but first we need to talk about rules.'

Antonia looked up and met his hazel eyes.

'Aye, aye, captain,' she muttered.

'You got it right, sport,' Jack announced. 'I can see you laughing at me now, but at sea, a crisis can blow up in seconds, and the captain is always in charge. While we're on board, you do what I say, when I say. Got it?'

The salt smell of the sea grew stronger as the dark outline of land dropped away behind them. Apart from the gurgle and slap of water, the Kingfisher was silent. Antonia had never been on such a small boat. They were so alone, and the starry sky was so vast above them that Antonia suddenly realised how much she needed Jack and his nautical skills.

'Aye, aye,' she whispered again.

Jack's hazel eyes scanned her face sharply, as if he were looking for traces of sarcasm, but he made no comment.

He lifted one tanned hand and began ticking off points on his fingers.

'In a minute, I'll show you where all the safety equipment is, but before you take another step on board — rule number one — no shoes on deck.'

He glared at her strappy sandals.

'You object to my shoes? They're Italian!'

Jack was unmoved.

'They're leaving marks on my planking, so off!'

Antonia cast a glance at his firm expression and slid off her beautiful shoes. She wriggled her feet experimentally.

'Naked toes!' she commented.

'Next,' Jack continued with his rules, 'I run a dry ship while we're at sea. Drink as much as you like in harbour, but no alcohol while we're under way.'

Antonia cocked an eyebrow.

'Does that rule apply to the captain?'

'I don't find it a problem,' Jack said loftily. 'Next, fresh water is rationed.

We'll stop off at Galliwasp Island and try to get more, but in the meantime, don't waste it!'

'Shower rather than bath?'

'Drinking only. You use sea water for everything else.'

Antonia blinked, but Jack looked so stern she decided to stay silent. He led her down below and gestured to the tiny, fitted kitchen behind them.

'The galley,' he told her. 'It'll be your turn every third day.'

'I thought slaves came with every charter,' Antonia muttered.

Then she wondered what she'd said to make Jack look so angry.

'This trip is your idea, so I'll be expecting you to pull your weight.'

Antonia's eyes opened wide.

'OK, OK,' she murmured.

Jack's eyes met hers without softening.

'This will be your bunk,' he snapped, gesturing to a space that ran along the underside of the boat.

'It looks more like a coffin than a

bedroom,' Antonia murmured doubtfully.

He placed his hands on his hips and talked down at her.

'If you don't like the facilities on board, why don't you nip back and charter the QE 2? One more whinge out of you, and I dump you.'

Antonia could see that he meant it. She limited her reply to a non-provocative, 'Sorry.'

He glared at her for a few seconds longer before saying, 'All right then. Go to bed. I'll sail the boat with Curly tonight. It's too dark to show you where everything is now, but in the morning you'll be working.'

He stalked away, leaving Antonia to discover that her bunk was stacked high with royal blue canvas bags that turned out to be full of spare sails.

'Call it another character-building experience,' she murmured, as she explored the unfamiliar confines of the boat.

The nautical equipment in the tiny

bathroom was all strange to her, but she was determined not to call Jack. She figured it out, washed in no more than one cup of water, unpacked her night things and cleared herself a space to sleep, feeling proud of herself because she didn't once have to ask for assistance.

The next morning, Jack was busy with maps and a bronze compass as she went up on deck. He looked engrossed, so Antonia went past him and stood by the rail of the yacht, holding her second cup of coffee. The complete absence of land was a shock as she looked around her. The horizon was absolutely clear and the sky was a circular blue vault above them. She inhaled the freshness and the cleanness and felt happy.

'Makes you glad to be alive, don't it?' a deep voice enquired from the middle of the boat.

Curly was sitting with his back comfortably on the mast, smiling at her with a friendly glint in his dark amber eyes. Antonia went over to him and sat down. He politely lowered the book he'd been reading. She read the title and felt very surprised.

'Chaucer?'

Curly looked amused.

'Don't you like him?'

'Well, we had the Canterbury Tales at school,' Antonia confessed frankly, 'but I never had the least idea what it was about.'

'You more scientific?'

'I'm more the decorative type,' she said, pulling a face.

'What for the good Lord give you brains?' Curly demanded. 'You waste your life,' he went on as if she bored him, and picked up his book once more.

Antonia regarded him curiously.

'Which island are you from?' she asked.

One eye came over the top of the book.

'A small one, just off the north coast of France.'

'Goodness! Do you ever get home?'

'I should visit my mother sometime, but I think of warm beer and English rain and I write her a letter.'

Antonia thought of dingy old London and looked around her at the sparkling blue day.

'It's 'way nicer at sea,' she admitted.

Stung by Curly's dismissal of her intellect, she hunted for something clever to say, something serious.

'What do you do for work? The unemployment must be terrible out here.'

Curly's mouth opened in a wide grin.

'On the contrary, people are so desperate for staff, they'd do anything to hire a good man. Just last night, I was press-ganged myself.'

Antonia slanted him a quick look.

'Sorry about the gun,' she muttered, feeling embarrassed. 'I'd never have used it.'

'No hard feelings.'

She looked again. The smile was still there.

'You mean it?'

Curly shrugged.

'Dames with guns, mobs bent on group surgery, life's never dull around Jack.'

'Goodness! You mean those men wanted to harm him?'

Curly nodded.

'No wonder he wanted to leave in a hurry,' Antonia said thoughtfully. 'What did he do?'

Curly smiled.

'It all started when Florentine Mills took a fancy to Jack.'

His smile grew broader.

'Then her husband's buddies got him all riled up.'

Antonia nodded understandingly.

'He wanted to stop Jack?'

Curly shook his head.

'Oh, no. He thought Jack should pay for the privilege.'

Antonia looked at the blue sea and blue sky. She truly was in a different world out here.

'Would Jack pay a woman?' she asked in a small voice.

'Don't you worry about Jack. He told Florentine there was no chance months ago. It was just rum firing up her family. Jack keeps to himself where women are concerned.'

'I am not in the least concerned with Jack's personal life,' Antonia said quickly. 'But surely we can't go back to Swimp Island now.'

Curly laughed.

'It'll blow over. Flo will start chasing someone else and the boys will whip up a new feud. That's the way it goes on the islands.'

He looked perfectly happy. Antonia was still curious about him.

'Did you meet Jack in London?' she asked.

'We met in a bar in Sydney,' Curly answered.

Jack had come up behind them. He took a seat on the hot deck next to Curly. His hazel eyes were full of light this morning, and there was a smile in them as he said to Antonia, 'More precisely, Curly was being helped out of

52

a bar in Sydney.'

Curly chuckled richly.

'Jack took a dislike to the bouncer's attitude, and we've been mates ever since.'

He looked at Antonia.

'Now, it's your turn to answer a few questions.'

'OK,' she said, sitting a little straighter, very aware of Jack's listening figure. 'Ask away.'

'What's with your brother, the one who's gone missing? He eccentric, or something?'

'You wouldn't think so,' Antonia said. 'He's an academic, and a bit dippy about anthropology, but otherwise he's the sanest person in my family.'

'Why did he go to Sugar Cay?'

'He wrote and said that the people who lived there were the direct descendants of the Ashanti people. He spent months in Africa studying their myths and legends.'

'So why study them again?' Jack demanded.

Antonia tried to sound informed.

'The stories have changed because of the move to the Caribbean,' she said uncertainly, and then with more confidence, 'and Max will write a book about it. That's what anthropologists do.'

Curly frowned.

'How come your family's not worried about him?'

'I am family,' Antonia pointed out.

'Male family,' Curly added.

She sniffed.

'Daddy lives in the country and thinks about nothing but raising chickens, and then shooting them. There's no-one else, really. Max's mother, my step-mother, ran off with a rally driver and left Max behind. He was just a youngster and we became ever so close, like a real brother and sister. We were brought up by a nanny.'

Antonia had a sudden vision of kindly Nanny Bates and the safe, secure world of the nursery. Her own mother had settled in Buenos Aries and had never sought to take charge of Antonia.

'She has to stay in bed now, because she's so old, but Max and I still visit her.'

Curly and Jack exchanged a glance. Antonia couldn't read the message that passed between them, but the look Jack turned on her was kinder than usual.

'So there's only you to find out the score with your brother?'

'Don't worry. If he's in trouble, we'll fix it,' Curly added.

Antonia felt a stir of happiness around her heart. Unlikely champions as the pair were, she felt better now she had someone on her side.

'Thank you,' she said, and her voice filled up with emotion. 'You don't know how much Max means to me.'

At the first threat of feminine tears, both males sprang to their feet.

'I don't suppose your nanny taught you how to cook, did she?' Curly asked, changing the subject.

'Safety drill comes first,' Jack interrupted, 'and then cleaning. I'll show you where to stow the sails we're not using, and then you can do your share of swabbing the deck and no whinging!'

'I never whinge,' Antonia said with dignity. 'Do you have any rubber gloves? I've left mine behind.'

'Sorry, princess,' Jack mocked, pushing a bucket full of cleaning equipment at her. 'You'll have to get your hands dirty.'

As Antonia began scrubbing the Kingfisher under Jack's supervision, she realised to her surprise that she was cleaning and polishing an already spotless boat. The woodwork glowed with layers of polish, the brass sparkled and gleamed, the portholes shone. Jack was fussy about tidiness, too, insisting that they turn out every locker and stow everything neatly.

'I'm surprised you two bachelors are so tidy,' Antonia mused as she scrubbed the already-shining cutlery with sea water and then polished each item before putting it away in the correct drawer.

'Have you never heard the expression shipshape?' Jack teased, his eyes smiling. 'A couple of hours a day, and the ship's right and tight. Come and help me start the engine, will you?'

Antonia was surprised.

'You've got an engine?'

'Sure, but why have the smelly thing running if we don't need it? We need to put some fuel in the tank, though. Think you can cope?'

Antonia did her best, but Jack turned around in time to see her struggling to extricate her hands from under a heavy drum of diesel. He frowned.

'You hurt yourself?'

'It's nothing,' Antonia said, hiding her hands behind her back.

Jack advanced on her, looking stern.

'You can't neglect even small scrapes in the tropics. Let me see.'

He took her small hands in his big tanned ones and looked them over with a puzzled expression.

'I can't see anything, but I heard you cry out in pain.'

Antonia felt a little breathless at his touch and the nearness of his body. Not trusting her voice, she silently extended her fingers. The three middle nails on her right hand were freshly torn and ragged. Jack looked scornful.

'You were yelling over a broken nail?'

'I didn't complain,' Antonia said quickly.

Jack didn't let go of her hand.

'They're just nails,' he said, almost to himself, still looking at her hand.

'They're not just nails!' Antonia cried, goaded by his dismissal. 'They are works of art! Look!'

She placed her left hand, the one with the undamaged nails, on top of Jack's large brown hand.

'I've been cultivating these for months.'

Jack's dark lashes flickered as he looked down at the smooth satin of her hand with its perfectly-shaped finger-nails. Her pale, slim fingers, and the rose-coloured ovals that tipped them, looked so feminine lying against the strong brown of his hand. Tension fizzed out of nowhere and built up behind them. Antonia tried to snatch back her hand, but Jack held it tightly, then he raised it to his lips and placed a gentle kiss on each finger. He looked up and met her eyes. There was a warm light in the hazel depths of his gaze.

'Give me your other hand,' he suggested softly. 'I'll kiss it better.'

'You are disgusting!' Antonia snapped.

She could still feel the imprint of his lips on her skin. Her own breath sounded loud in her ears, and she was afraid that Jack would hear the uncertain shake in her voice. She took refuge in snobbishness.

'You're a hired man, not my lover.'

Hurt flashed across Jack's face for a moment, then vanished, replaced by anger.

'Didn't take you long to throw that in my face,' he drawled.

He turned away and climbed up the ladder that led from the cabin to the deck. Antonia was left looking at his

59

disappearing denim shorts, strong legs and bare feet as he ascended, wishing she could undo what she'd just said. Feeling rather ashamed of herself, she worked on until everything in the galley sparkled. Then, because she felt grubby after her efforts, she creamed her face and rubbed her hands with cologne, then she combed her hair. It was already looking dull because she couldn't wash it, so she decided to plait it back out of the way rather than leave it loose.

Then she changed into buttercup-yellow linen shorts and a clean blouse. She still didn't feel ready to face Jack, so she re-did her make-up and then sat on one of the bench seats next to the table, the only table. You couldn't avoid a person in the small space of a forty-foot boat. Better get it over with. She climbed the ladder up to the dazzling blue world on deck. Jack was balancing a polished brass contraption on the boat rails and squinting into the sun. Hoping that he wasn't a man to bear grudges, Antonia approached him curiously.

'What are you doing?'

'Taking a noon sight,' he said. 'I'll teach you how to navigate if you like.'

'Oh, you don't need to bother,' Antonia told him brightly. 'I have a SatNav in my bag.'

Glad to be able to contribute something she dived into her handbag and fetched out the portable unit.

'Isn't it dinky?' she said, offering the tiny, electronic gadget to Jack. 'The man in the shop said I'd never get lost with this.'

Jack used a thick pencil to mark his map before looking at her with barely-concealed impatience.

'Did the man in the shop happen to tell you how to go on if the battery ran out?'

'No,' Antonia faltered, looking down at the gadget.

She shaded the read-out on the tiny screen. It was showing their position in degrees. Latitude and longitude, it said.

Jack despised her anyway, so she might as well make a clean breast of it. She looked up and met his eyes bravely.

'I don't have the first clue what this degree stuff means anyway,' she confessed.

Jack's thick dark lashes swept shut briefly and then opened as he raised his eyes to heaven. He took a deep breath and opened his mouth. Antonia had an idea that what Jack was about to roar at her was going to be less than complimentary, but Curly came sauntering over to them, and Jack shut his mouth with a snap. Curly seemed completely unaware of the tension between her and Jack.

'Those little navigation gadgets, they're OK,' he told Antonia. 'We carry one ourselves, but only as a back-up.'

His gaze met hers and there was a definite smile in the depths of it.

'Best to learn traditional navigation then you can't ever be lost.'

He handed her a battered, large-format paperback book. Jack swung off to the front of the boat and Curly continued on his way, leaving Antonia alone in the bright sunshine. She looked down at the book in her hand. It was called, *A Beginner's Guide to Navigation*.

Jack had gone to the front of the boat, yanking at a horrible mass of tangled, nylon fishing line. He didn't even know why he was bothering. Two other lines trailed behind in the creamy bubbling wake of the boat, but not a fish had they caught yet. He tugged at a particularly stubborn knot and growled to himself.

It was probably a good thing Curly had stopped him roaring at Antonia. She had more or less chartered the boat, and it would be better if he didn't upset her. The ignorance of her, though! The stupidity of some people never ceased to amaze Jack. Antonia was stumbling around the Caribbean with no more idea of how to go on than a day-old kitten.

He looked back along the boat. She

was sitting on the wooden deck in the small patch of shade cast by the sails. She'd pushed her plait over one shoulder, and she was frowning over early pages of the navigation book. As Jack watched, the tip of a pink tongue popped out of the corner of her mouth. He felt his lips lift in a smile.

She was cute, there was no getting away from it. He was beginning to think that Antonia, with her fashion outfits, her perfectly-groomed exterior and her killing air of innocent self-possession, was the most attractive woman he'd ever come across. But the last thing he wanted in his life was a female who, while she might be kind of fun and was certainly very decorative, was also young, vulnerable and definitely in need of looking after. If only I was alone, Jack thought, yearning for a solo voyage.

Then he remembered that the first few times he'd gone out alone in the Kingfisher, he'd thought he was going to die in the middle of the ocean. He'd made it home by sheer luck, and he'd surprised himself when he went back for more. But from the moment he'd seen the Kingfisher abandoned in a Sydney boatyard, she'd been his boat.

The innate stubbornness that had driven him into learning how to restore her, by a process of trial and error rather than pay the experts, had driven him on until he'd mastered the art of sailing. But it had never been much fun until he'd teamed up with Curly. People needed people. He padded across the warm wooden deck to Antonia, hoping that she didn't bear grudges.

'How you getting on?' he asked her.

She looked up at him and shaded her eyes against the sun.

'Perfectly,' she told him.

'Good-oh,' Jack said.

He couldn't think what to say next, so he decided to walk on by and see how Curly was doing, but Antonia stopped him. She looked up at him with the hint of a laugh in her big round eyes.

'Wait a minute, Jack. You know, you haven't told me about yourself. What made you take to sea?'

Jack was surprised by an urge to share his story with her, but he crushed it. Start telling your secrets to a woman and you'd be in real trouble. Love them and leave them, that was his motto. He never told anyone about the misery of being an unwanted, fostered child, but he almost told Antonia that, while the senior partners of the law firm he worked for had been reluctant to let him go at first, they'd finally agreed to a sabbatical.

'Get this sailing madness out of your system,' he'd been told.

The office had promptly started a book on how long he'd last at sea. Jack had heard that most bets were on him trailing home in under six weeks. Instead, after only a month, he'd sent in his permanent resignation. He'd never been back, and he'd never wanted to.

'Is your past life a secret?' Antonia asked.

She looked cute as a button, sitting there in her neat little outfit and smiling her innocent smile, but Jack hardened his heart and reminded himself once again that she was a wealthy woman and he'd better not forget it. The rich were different, he knew that, and he'd sworn to have nothing to do with them.

A picture flashed into his mind of a young man wearing a designer suit with a twenty-thousand dollar watch on his wrist. The man was sitting at the best table of the best restaurant in Sydney, and across from him sat the fabulous blonde daughter of the richest family in Australia. Even the sophisticated patrons of the restaurant were looking at him with envy.

But what they didn't know was that this beautiful woman was planning to have her ailing father declared mentally unfit, and, once she had him locked away, she wanted to use this bright young lawyer to obtain as much money as possible out of her family trust. And instead of being shocked, that young man was gleefully thinking how well his career was going to do out of this case. Jack knew only too well just how despicable some of the rich were, because he'd been that young lawyer.

Antonia's gaze was still fixed on him, waiting for an answer. Jack looked down at her thoughtfully for a moment longer and then he grinned.

'Let's just say that the law was about to ruin my life,' he told her.

She could interpret that any way she chose, he told himself, smiling.

5

For the next few days, life on board the Kingfisher was peaceful. The sun shone every day, the wind blew in the right direction, and once the daily drills and chores were done, Antonia found it most enjoyable to sit on the deck and listen to the waves slap and gurgle against the front of the boat.

Sometimes she read, sometimes she just looked at the view, and sometimes she took a nap. She was never left alone to sail the boat, but she stayed awake for one of the night watches, if only to keep the men company. She thought they appreciated it, and she felt as if she were getting the hang of life at sea.

One afternoon, as she sat half-reading, half-dozing, Jack jumped straight over her. She looked up from her book of navigation. He was grabbing at one of the ropes that let the sails go up and down.

'Excuse me!' she cried, half-laughing, half-annoyed.

He turned to her with a face that was set and serious.

'Put on your safety harness, now!' he ordered.

Canvas flapped as he dropped the entire main sail without bothering to furl it or fasten it inside its bag. Reacting as much to the authority in his voice as his words, Antonia scrambled down the ladder, flung her book on the table, and ran to the locker where the webbing harnesses were kept.

Thanks to Jack's drills, she had no trouble getting into one, although her fingers were shaking and the butterflies in her stomach were the worst she'd ever had. As the last buckle on the harness clipped shut, Antonia looked up. The light that was filtering through the cabin portholes was dimming by the second, turning from light blue to dark blue, to black. A wind that had blown out of nowhere howled in the metal stays of the mast. The boat lurched violently downwards, and then seemed to stand up with its nose in the air.

It's a hurricane, Antonia thought. Her first impulse was to hide in her bunk, but she squashed her cowardly feelings and picked up two more safety harnesses instead. Jack and Curly might need them. It seemed incredible that only a few minutes ago the Kingfisher had been floating peacefully through blue seas. Now she rolled violently as Antonia tried to walk up the aisle of the cabin and the motion threw her from side to side, bruising her arms as she climbed up the ladder.

Outside in the cockpit, Curly was fighting with the big, wooden steering-wheel of the ship. Antonia screamed out loud as she caught the full force of the wind. If Curly heard her, he didn't turn around. The boat pitched and tossed. Huge waves crashed over the rails of the boat, flooding the deck. Antonia tapped Curly on the shoulder and offered him a safety harness. He flashed her a quick grin and he patted his chest. He was already wearing one. His attention went straight back to the steering.

Antonia looked around for Jack. He was standing at the front of the boat, leaning out into the pounding waves. Antonia gripped the top rung of the boat rail for safety and squinted hard to see what he was doing. He was leaning over the rail, pulling on something. Wet canvas lay on the deck behind him. As the boat keeled over to one side, Antonia saw more wet canvas tossing around in the heaving seas. It was the big sail she'd learned to call a spinnaker. Jack must have dropped it so quickly it had gone in the ocean, and now he was trying to get it back.

She hesitated for a second. The boat was lurching around like a mad thing, and the wind that screamed past her ears was truly frightening, but she also knew that the spinnaker was a difficult sail for one person to pull in alone, so she took a deep breath and told herself to go to help him at once. She was afraid to let go of the rail, so she held on to it tight and shuffled sideways along the side of the boat.

She'd only taken a few steps when the Kingfisher seemed to fall over sideways, towards Antonia. The rail she was holding disappeared so far down under the raging water that she saw her hands disappear into the ocean. Desperately afraid that the boat would drag her under, Antonia let go. She tried to take a step back towards the cockpit, where she could just see Curly straining to hold the wheel, but water sucked at her ankles and dragged her down.

'I'm drowning!' she screamed, but her cry was lost in the wind.

Then, miraculously, the Kingfisher began to right herself.

Water drained over Antonia's feet and swirled into the ocean as first the deck and then the boat rail appeared out of the sea. She stood there, shaking. She didn't know what to do. It seemed impossible that she could ever make her way to the front of the boat to help

Jack. Perhaps she'd better go back and go below. Her mind felt fuzzy. It was hard to make a decision.

Antonia looked from the front of the boat to the back, wondering what she should do, and it was then she saw the wave. A great, blue-grey wall of glassy water towered over the Kingfisher, like the Empire State Building was falling towards her like a bad dream. Antonia's knees went weak. She knew it would hit her, but what could she do? Nothing but take a deep breath and remember the prayers that Nanny Bates had taught her.

At the exact second the wave slapped up against her and swept her into the water, Antonia remembered that, while she had put on her safety harness, she had forgotten to clip it to anything. She felt herself tossed overboard as if she were somersaulting and then she was thrown violently into the sea. It was warmer under the water than it had been outside, but Antonia tasted salt water in her mouth and knew she was going to die.

Her eyes were screwed tight shut and her body fell first one way and then the other. The world was shaking her like she was the olive in a cocktail. She didn't even know which way was up, so there was no point trying to swim to the surface. And if she got there, what then?

The Kingfisher would have been carried away by the wind, and Jack and Curly had all they could do to stop the boat capsizing. They wouldn't be able to come back for her for hours, maybe days, and by then the sharks would have got her.

But even as Antonia's brain hummed with panicky, despairing thoughts, her body obeyed its deeply-buried survival mechanism. Her eyes opened, and despite the blurring and stinging of salt water, she could see the lighter water of the surface above her, which meant she must be looking upwards. Her legs kicked strongly and her hands swept up and she swam as never before.

She thought she'd never make it. Her

lungs were burning and convulsing with the need for oxygen, but just as she was about to give in and breathe water, her head popped out into the open. Antonia opened her mouth and gulped in air. Tropical rain was now falling all around her. The big drops hissed as they hit the huge, rolling waves. She took in another breath and pushed her wet hair out of her eyes. She could see nothing over the grey-blue mountains of water around her. She was alone in the ocean. She ought to try to swim to the top of one of the waves and see if she could see the Kingfisher, but right now that seemed beyond her. It was all she could do to tread water and breathe.

Then she felt a violent knock on her shoulder. A shark, her mind screamed! She turned slowly in the water, dreading what she was going to see, but there, to her utter amazement, was Jack. His hair was slicked down by the water, and curled thickly under his ears. He seemed to bob high in the water because he was lifted by the orange lifejacket he was wearing.

Incredibly, he was laughing. His hazel eyes gleamed. His white teeth flashed in his tan face, and he seemed unconcerned by the rain that ran down his face. Antonia wanted to throw herself at him. She swam clumsily through the water and flung her arms around his neck.

'Jack!'

'Don't choke me!'

He held out a life ring.

'Let's get this over your head.'

Antonia didn't want to take her fingers out of the safety of his wet shirt, but eventually Jack managed to get the ring over her head.

'You can let go!' he bawled. 'We're roped together now.'

Antonia could see the wet ropes that trailed in the heaving water all around them, but she still didn't want to let go of Jack. She could feel the buoyancy of the ring, and that made her feel confident enough to let go with one hand. The other one she kept firmly twisted in the shoulder of his shirt. The waves still heaved and tossed around them, and she couldn't bear the thought of being separated.

'This way!' Jack shouted in her ear.

He began swimming sideways, moving awkwardly under the orange lifejacket, ropes trailing through the water behind him. She'd hold him back if she didn't let go. Antonia released her hold on his shirt and began to swim herself. She didn't ask where they were going, or why they were swimming. She was content to follow Jack.

Vibration in the water ahead of them made her look up. She could see the white hull of the Kingfisher about twenty feet away. Antonia trod water and watched the boat. She looked enormous from this angle, and she was pitching up and down in the heavy swell. At least the rain had stopped, and the wind had gone. Jack seemed to be communicating with hand signals, and Antonia caught a glimpse of Curly's dark figure as the angle of the boat changed. Then there was a tug on the rope attached to her life ring and Jack was treading water behind her.

'Get ready to reach for the ladder,' he shouted. 'Now, go on! Swim!'

As they swam towards Kingfisher, Antonia thought that she'd never dare try to climb on to it. Even though the yacht had a ladder running down the back into the water, the heavy waves were making the boat leap up and then crash down in a way that was truly terrifying. The throb of the engine got louder as they got closer. Antonia's heart was racing faster than the engine.

'Now!' Jack shouted.

To her amazement her fingers connected with the cold metal of the ladder and she managed to haul herself up on to the first rung. She felt a push from below as Jack put his arms under her ring, and gave her such a strong boost that she practically flew up the rest of the ladder. She tipped over the edge of the boat and lay in the cockpit gasping.

A few white clouds hid the sun, but

the wind and rain had completely gone, and she could feel the tropical warmth returning. She heard metal jingling as Jack climbed up the ladder. He jumped into the cockpit and began taking off the lifejacket and then his safety harness. Once he was free of the restricting equipment, he made quickly to Antonia and leaned over her, concern in his deep hazel eyes.

'Are you OK?'

'I think so!' she replied.

Her heartbeat slowed and she started to feel more normal. She followed Jack's example, sitting up and wriggling out of the ropes and straps and buoyancy aids that surrounded her. She looked up and met his worried eyes. The sun came out behind her and lit his face. She could see gold sparks in the brown of his irises.

'I really think so!' she repeated. 'I'm so surprised to find myself breathing! I thought for sure I'd die in that hurricane!'

Jack kneeled back on his heels and

gave a great guffaw of laughter.

'Hurricane! That was no hurricane! That was just a little tropical squall. It was nothing.'

'You have to be joking!' Antonia said, but as she looked around her, she could see that the sky was clear blue once again.

The waves were already smoothing themselves out. It was a perfectly calm, tropical day. She swung back and met Jack's eyes in amazement.

'You mean it's all over?'

His smile was warm.

'Until the next one.'

Curly stayed at the wheel while Jack went into the cabin. The sound of the engine died away. He came back whistling.

'Antonia, go below and dry off. I've put the kettle on. Be sure to drink some tea now. You've had a shock.'

Antonia looked at Curly and then at Jack.

'You guys saved my life,' she said quietly.

'All part of the service.'

Jack grinned, waving an airy hand.

'All our tours come with a near-death experience,' Curly joked. 'It's included in the price.'

It didn't feel like a joke to Antonia as she slipped down the ladder and rummaged in her bunk for a towel and dry clothes. She still had no idea how the men had managed to control the boat and go back for her in such dreadful weather. She'd been incredibly lucky, and she knew it. If Jack and Curly had been slower off the mark, or less skilled in their handling of the boat . . .

When the kettle whistled, she got out the battered silver teapot and made enough tea for three people. She turned the gas off very carefully. It made her wince to think how bored she'd been by Jack's lectures on the right way to use gas at sea.

'I'll never grumble about his safety drills again,' she promised.

She poured out three mugs of tea

and took two of them on deck. It was impossible to believe that they'd just been in a storm. The weather was blue perfection, and calm enough for the Kingfisher to be now back on autopilot. Jack and Curly had put the main sail up and were now busily coiling ropes and folding sails, tidying up the boat.

Antonia went back into the cabin and picked up her hot drink. She must have been a different person when she'd first got on the boat and complained about the thickness of the mugs and the blackness of the tea, because she now felt as if she was drinking nectar! She drank her tea slowly, savouring every mouthful, then rinsed the mug in sea water. Maybe she had been a different person. Something had changed, that was for sure.

She didn't want to think about it. Antonia jumped up and decided to tidy the cabin. The storm had thrown the boat around so violently that even Jack's careful stowage had come undone in places. Antonia worked quickly, closing doors that had flown open, repacking the packets of instant dried noodles that had scattered themselves around the cabin and then turning her attention to the bookshelf.

She tightened the stretchy cord that ran across the front of the books and began to replace the volumes that had fallen out — books about sailing; books about fishing; books about marine life in all its forms; a book about corporate law.

Corporate law?

Curious, Antonia opened the volume. A sheaf of heavy papers fell out on to the bench seat. A few fell on the floor. Antonia bent and picked them up, leafing through them with a growing feeling of disbelief. She looked up as Jack's tanned legs, then the rest of him, appeared down the ladder. Dressed in nothing but a layer of suntan, wet shorts and a soggy safari shirt, he looked every inch the beach bum, but she had the evidence right in her hands. She met Jack's eyes accusingly.

'You were a lawyer!'

His brown gaze was rueful.

'I try to keep it a secret.'

Antonia looked at his strong face and wondered how she'd missed the intelligence that clearly lived there.

'I can't figure you out.'

He shrugged.

'You're not supposed to. I'm just the hired man.'

Antonia met his clear brown gaze.

'I should never have said that. I'm sorry.'

The boat was rocking slightly more than usual in the aftermath of the squall, but warm blue light was pouring through the portholes, and the glint of moving water flickered gold on the polished wood of the cabin fittings. Jack stood in front of her, watching her face intently.

'No wonder I trusted you,' she said softly, half to herself.

He took a swift step towards her. One of his hands went under her chin, tipping it up, forcing her to look at him.

'Don't trust me!' he said, and his voice was low and harsh. 'I tried to run off with your money, remember?'

Antonia tried to shake her head, but his hand restrained her. The emotion that was unfurling inside her had a depth and painful sweetness that was new to her, and yet she recognised it at once. Jack's eyes shone amber like a lion's as they caught the sunlight. She met them openly.

'You took money for a voyage, and here we are.'

His hand left her chin and fell to her shoulder. His grip was painful as he shook her.

'Only because you outsmarted me!'

Antonia smiled at the memory. Setting out on this voyage had been crazy, but somehow she'd known it was the right thing to do. Just as she now knew that the right thing to do was to lift one hand to Jack's face and touch his cheek gently. She saw his throat move as he made a harsh sound and reached for her as though he was trying

86

to prove something.

His lips touched hers with such a deep and unbelievable force that Antonia felt a whole explosion in her mind. She leaned closer towards the heat of his body and wound her arms around his neck. Jack broke the contact between them. His tone was low and intense.

'You'd be a fool to come anywhere near me, Antonia. We both know that I tried to take your money.'

Antonia's fingers went to her freshly-kissed lips and traced the delicious sensation that Jack's touch had left.

'You didn't take anything,' she said to him softly, boldly.

The answering fire in his eyes told her that he knew she wasn't talking about money. But then a steel shutter seemed to come down over his eyes and shut him away from her.

'Jack,' Antonia breathed, touching his arm. 'Jack can't we — '

His mouth seemed to fold up and go hard.

'No!'

He held up a hand to stop her from saying more.

'Listen!'

He tipped his head towards a faint sound.

'Curly's shouting,' he told her in a gruff voice. 'We must see what he wants.'

Antonia couldn't move. His big hands went to her upper arms, lifting her aside so that he could squeeze past her and go up on deck. She followed him. She understood that it was important to see what Curly wanted. And maybe it was as well they'd been interrupted.

On deck, she could see at once that there was no emergency. Curly and Jack stood at the front of the boat, pointing and laughing.

'What is it?' Antonia asked, shading her eyes from the sun with a hand and looking out in the same direction as the men.

Jack turned a laughing face towards her.

'You'll see in a minute. There!'

'Wow!' Antonia screamed. 'Dolphins!'

Three perfectly-curved backs broke from the sea and plunged down again in a crystal spray of water. Then another dolphin burst out of the sea and spun on its tail in a giddy whirl. Another team broke through the waves and somersaulted in formation. Antonia grabbed Jack's arm and laughed out loud. As he smiled back at her, his brown eyes reflected his pleasure in the experience they were sharing.

'Such acrobatics. It's as though they were trained!'

Jack threw his head back and laughed out loud in the sunlight.

'Dolphins love to play. They do this all the time,' he told her. 'Fancy a swim?'

She felt a strong reluctance to get back in the water that had so nearly killed her.

'What about sharks?'

'Dolphins chase them away. We'll be all right.'

Jack peeled off his shirt and his shorts, so that he stood on the deck wearing only swimming trunks. Antonia looked away, and then peeked back. He was so good looking. His whole body was as fit and as supple as if he worked out every day. Antonia suddenly realised that the boat was like a gym. At first the mechanical effort of winching up sails and dealing with ropes had been hard for her, but now she was nearly as fit and supple as Jack.

She heard a great splash and realised that Curly was already in the water. She saw him kicking out joyously, heading away from the yacht.

'What if the boat sails away without us?'

'Sea anchor,' Jack replied, then dived neatly from the side of the boat and into the water, hardly rippling the surface.

Antonia hesitated a moment longer, then she scrambled down the ladder into the hot cabin and started hunting for a swimsuit. She didn't feel up to diving from the side of the boat. Instead she stepped cautiously down the metal ladder at the back of the Kingfisher. Jack was treading water.

'What took you so long?' he demanded.

'I had to decide what to wear.'

Jack rolled his eyes to heaven.

'The dolphins won't care!'

Antonia didn't want him to despise her. She flicked back her fringe and looked at him earnestly, willing him to understand.

'How can it be a perfect moment if I'm wearing the wrong thing?'

Jack seemed about to laugh, but then he looked at her slim body in the lime-green swimsuit she had chosen and his eyes expressed appreciation as well as understanding. Antonia suppressed an urge to kiss him.

'Where are the dolphins?' she asked, still on the ladder.

'Get in the water. They'll come visiting if they feel like it.'

Antonia lowered herself in. The water

was cool and delicious. A pair of warm arms circled her from behind.

'It's best to swim again,' Jack told her gently, as he drew her into the haven of his broad chest. 'It's like getting on a horse after a fall.'

Antonia realised that he had understood the fear that had plagued her as she entered the water again. She felt fine now, because she was supported by Jack. She lay cradled in his arms, rocking with the smooth swell that lifted them gently up, and then softly down. Within a few minutes, long, torpedo-shaped fish appeared in the water around them.

'I've never been so close to a wild creature!' she whispered, entranced, looking at the friendly faces of the dolphins.

Their snouts seemed to be smiling at her, and there was definitely curiosity in their deep, liquid dark eyes. Jack gave her a grin and swam away. At once a dolphin swam to join him. Jack opened his legs wide in the water. The dolphin swam through them and then jumped out of the water in a joyous arc, landing with a great splash.

Antonia could have sworn that the big fish was laughing at Jack as it looked back at him with intelligence shining from its eyes. She stayed close to the Kingfisher, nervously treading water, occasionally putting out a hand to touch the wild creatures that swam past her.

Jack was completely at home, Antonia thought, watching him play tag with the dolphin. He was as free as the sea creatures themselves, as wild as the seagulls that flew overhead calling loudly of adventure and freedom. Yet he never went far away from her. She was aware of his watchful gaze upon her, and after giving her a few minutes to get used to the situation, he came back to her and towed her farther out into the water. Antonia felt safe with him beside her. She cast off all caution and played freely in the salt water, relishing being fit, alive and supremely happy.

She couldn't remember ever having such a good time before, not even when she was shopping!

After about an hour, the dolphins seemed to hear a mysterious call. They all turned in perfect formation and swam out into the deep ocean, keeping their places like a well-drilled flight team.

'There goes our shark patrol! Everybody back on the boat!' Jack shouted, obeying his own order.

'I'm starving,' Antonia cried, hauling herself on board.

'And it's your turn to pour water on the noodles,' Curly reminded her. Groaning, Antonia went below.

6

Early the next morning, while she was cleaning the cabin, Antonia heard Curly shouting. When she went up on deck, it took her a few moments to spot him. He'd shinned up the main mast and was clinging to the top of it like a monkey.

'Land!' he shouted.

Antonia shaded her eyes.

'I can't see anything.'

Jack came up behind her. His touch on her bare arm made her shiver as he gently turned her to look in the right direction.

'See that cloud on the horizon?' he told her. 'Keep watching and it'll turn into rock.'

Antonia couldn't see anything, but suddenly she took a deep breath.

'I can smell it! Coconuts and green things.'

She sniffed again.

'I never knew earth had a smell.'

'Some people can navigate by scent,' Jack said, a smile in his eyes for her excitement. 'There are other signs as well. Those seabirds over there never go far from land, and how about that for a clue? A cigarette packet floating past us.'

Within an hour they were gliding past a white, sugar-sand beach, fringed by palm trees. Jack said that the water was deep enough to moor at the long black rickety dock that ran out to sea. Jack showed Antonia how to hang protective buoys over the Kingfisher's sides before he tied up. They dropped the last sail and stowed it neatly. Then they were free to jump out.

The jetty was no more than loose boards balanced on pilings. The rough wood planks were warm under Antonia's feet.

'My shoes!' she gasped. 'I nearly went ashore without shoes!'

'I don't think anyone on Galliwasp

Island will notice,' Jack said, smiling, but she rushed down below to hunt out a pair of sandals that matched her outfit exactly!

A large man in a Hawaiian shirt was sauntering along the jetty to meet them, smiling from under his straw hat.

'You folks want water?' he asked them.

Antonia ran up the ladder.

'Does that mean I can wash my hair?'

Jack haggled with the man before answering, then he turned to her with a smile in his eyes.

'Happy days!' he announced. 'From now on, you can have one cup of water to rinse with.'

Antonia felt obliged to offer to help with the water, but she was very pleased when the men said that they could manage without her. She left them rolling big drums along the dock and went below feeling excited. Clean hair at last! Until the water-loading was finished, she sat on the side of the boat letting her hair dry in the sun. As they walked along the jetty to the shore, Jack flipped a dark tress.

'Happy now?'

There was sarcastic inflection to his question, but Antonia noticed that his gaze kept going to the mass that floated around her shoulders.

There was a wooden shack near the beach that proclaimed **Store and Ships' Chandlers**. When they went inside it smelled of dried fish and engine oil. The same man who'd sold them the drinking water served them with packets of noodles.

'Don't you have anything fresh?' Antonia asked.

His eyes went to her, and then stayed fastened to her, lingering on her dark blond-streaked hair as if he hadn't noticed her before.

'There's a market in the village,' he answered absently, still looking at her before he turned to Jack. 'Is this woman yours?'

Antonia felt Jack's hand grab her wrist and squeeze it hard.

'She's with us,' he answered.

The man turned around to take a packet of dried soup from a dirty box and Jack whispered in her ear, 'I know what you're thinking, but honey, he's not the type to understand an independent woman.'

'Maybe I could make him understand,' Antonia muttered angrily, glaring at the man's back.

Jack looked down on her, smiling.

'It's your hair.'

He touched a thick strand gently.

'It's so beautiful. I can't keep my eyes off it myself.'

Jack's eyes were so warm and admiring, that Antonia felt dizzy. Before she could think of a reply, the shopkeeper had found the soup and was making up their bill. Jack moved forward to pay it.

'By the way,' Jack said casually, counting out his money, 'you seen anything of an anthropologist who's working on Sugar Cay? His name is Maximilian Everett-Cox.'

The shopkeeper seemed to freeze for a moment. Antonia saw the whites of his eyes as his eyes rolled in a startled look. Then the man collected himself and gave a casual shrug.

'I stick to my own island.'

Jack dropped his change into his pocket and picked up the stores.

'Just thought I'd ask.'

'Sure,' the big man said casually, but Antonia thought that he was watching them with an interest that amounted to fervour in his black eyes.

The light outside was blinding after the dark interior of the stuffy shop.

'That was not real retail therapy,' Antonia remarked. 'I want to look around the market.'

'I'll take the tucker back,' Jack said, hoisting the box on his shoulder.

'Jack, did you notice anything strange about that man?'

'Strange?'

'He looked very startled when you asked him about Max, and then he stared and stared at us.'

100

'I didn't notice a thing. Did you, Curly?'

Curly shook his head.

'Nah. Think I'll go swimming.'

He sauntered off in the direction of the beach. Two very pretty girls were sitting on the white sand, smiling at him.

Antonia still wasn't happy. She touched Jack's warm arm.

'I've got butterflies,' she told him.

He looked down at her in bewilderment.

'What does that mean?'

'There's something fishy about that guy. I know it. Don't you believe me?'

'Go shopping,' he told her, before turning round and striding off towards the jetty, still carrying the box on his shoulder.

Antonia felt an urge to run after him and make him understand, but something told her she was wasting her time.

Jack couldn't resist turning around to watch Antonia tripping down the path that led to the village, and the market.

$$101$$

He knew for a fact that she'd been washing in sea water all week, yet she was as sleek and as groomed as a racehorse, or maybe something more colourful, like a humming-bird. Her trim figure disappeared around a bend in the path, and Jack stepped out on to the jetty, watching the loose boards carefully.

It was uncanny how well she fitted in now. Jack felt as if she'd always been on the Kingfisher, and he admired her for the way she pulled her weight. He still wouldn't trust her to sail alone, but she turned out for her share of the night watches, and she was learning fast. She was even picking up navigation. In a few more weeks she'd be able to . . . Jack hesitated.

He meant that she'd be able to pick up her brother and fly home, Jack reminded himself as he heaved the box of supplies on deck. Don't you go getting used to that little lady. In a few days' time she'd be sitting in a first-class airliner, and not long after that she wouldn't even remember what the Kingfisher looked like, let alone how to sail her. And he and Curly could go back to their bachelor existence. Wouldn't that be nice?

Jack threw the box of food down the ladder to the cabin. He followed it down, but then gave the upturned box a kick. He'd put the stupid stuff away later. It was hot and boring in the cabin. He scrambled up the ladder. He'd walk into the village and see if Antonia had bought the place up.

As he was stepping off the end of the jetty on to the hot sand, Jack saw a furtive movement behind the ships' chandlers. A hand-painted **Back in Ten Minutes** sign had been propped up against the closed door. The guy was probably going for lunch. Jack looked at his watch. It was too early for lunch.

Jack wandered towards the store and then stopped and looked around him. The cove was deserted. The palm trees rustled gently over an empty white beach. Blue waves lapped at the shore, hissing in the hot, Caribbean sun. Antonia was paranoid. The shopkeeper had probably slipped away for an innocent cool drink. He'd be back any moment.

Jack hesitated for a moment longer, then slipped behind the wooden building. A very faint path ran through the sand towards the coarse grass that grew along the sea shore. Not even sure why he was doing it, Jack followed the path over the dunes and into the coconut plantations. He felt a bit stupid, ducking behind palm trees as he went, but the hot, heavy silence of the jungle made him want to stay out of sight.

The shopkeeper's tropical shirt was easy to follow. It soon became clear that he wasn't going somewhere close for a drink. Jack kept on following him, even if he wasn't sure why. The path was definitely leading them upwards. It turned and ran along the edge of a stream, or what would be a stream in the rainy season. Now it was full of smooth, round boulders with only a suggestion of dampness along the bottom.

The path twisted and Jack caught a glimpse of the shopkeeper's face. It was shiny and covered with sweat. He was breathing in a distressed way that made it clear he was not taking this walk for fun. Jack drew back under the shelter of some ferns. What was the guy doing?

The last section of the path was so steep that Jack had to scramble, using both hands to pull himself up. Once he got to the top he had to duck his head down quickly. He was on top of an open shelf of rock with no cover. He moved cautiously to the left, where a low-growing clump of bushes offered some cover. He eased himself into the middle of the bushes and then parted the stems carefully and looked out.

The man had thrown himself on the ground and was breathing in heavy gasps, recovering from the climb. It was a good five minutes before he rolled over and sat up. Then he reached into the breast pocket of his shirt and pulled out a mobile phone! Jack could have kicked himself. So much for Antonia and her suspicions. The top of the hill was probably the only place to get a good signal. The guy was going to ring his sister, or his mother, that was all.

'Three of them, boss, asking questions,' his voice came.

Jack's grip on the bush stems tightened. The shopkeeper was using a heavy dialect that was difficult to follow, but those words had been clear enough. Jack tilted his head and listened hard. The man seemed to be trying to get out of something. He was shaking his head, frowning.

'Boss, I don't know how to do that.'

The shopkeeper held his phone at a distance away from his ear. Either he didn't like what he was hearing or the person on the other end was shouting, or both.

'Man, that's heavy stuff,' he whined.

And then he seemed to quiver all over.

'No, no, I ain't arguing with you.'

106

He was holding the phone closer to his ear now, and his body was tense.

'Why, sure, it's an accident that happens all the time. But how — '

Jack leaned dangerously far out of the bushes and wished he could just catch what the voice on the other end of the phone was saying. The boss had obviously carried his point. The shop-keeper was nodding slowly.

'All right, I'll do that for you, man.'

He switched off his phone and stowed it away in his pocket. Too late Jack realised that, while he'd been straining to hear, he'd let his body come too far out of the bushes. He felt dangerously exposed, but it was prob-ably better to keep still. A flicker of movement now might draw the man's attention.

The shopkeeper stood quite still in the middle of the rocky opening for a few seconds longer. Then he shrugged his big shoulders and started for the path with a heavy tread. Jack cringed back as the man got close to him, but the shopkeeper was oblivious to his surroundings. His eyes were blank and he looked like a man who'd had a bad shock. As he walked close by, he launched himself down the path without even glancing in Jack's direction.

Jack waited until the sounds of the shopkeeper going down the path got far away, then let go of the bush stems and stretched his arms over his head. They were aching with the strain. Then he sat up and hugged his knees.

Three people asking questions, the man had said. And he had agreed to create an accident for his boss, one that he clearly didn't fancy arranging. The idea had left him looking sick and worried.

Jack got to his feet and swung himself lightly down the steep hillside. It was time to find Curly.

★ ★ ★

It was mid-afternoon before Antonia tripped along the jetty that led to the

108

Kingfisher. A train of small children followed her, grinning and chattering. Each one carried a box or a bundle or a big tin. Jack's head shot over the side of the Kingfisher and scowled at them.

'You opening a Sunday school?'

'Chill out, dude,' Antonia teased.

To her surprise no answering smile appeared in Jack's eyes.

'Get them out of here,' he growled and planted his fists on his waist and yelled at the kids. 'Stop right there! No-one goes on board.'

The children halted and looked up at Jack with big eyes. Then, recognising the mood he was in, they moved behind the shelter of Antonia.

'You are 'way ungrateful,' she told him, feeling puzzled by his bad temper. 'Look how much they carried for me.'

'Drop it on the jetty and scoot,' Jack ordered.

The kids understood his tone if not the words. Bright smiles dimmed and they silently deposited their various loads on to the warm wooden planking.

A few of the smallest started to slink away.

'Wait a minute!' Antonia cried.

She looked up at Jack's unforgiving figure.

'I promised them.'

She kicked off her shoes, swung up on deck and slipped down the ladder to where her luggage was stowed. Five minutes later the children were running down the jetty screaming with joy over their loot — ribbons, pencils and hair slides for the girls; combs, pens and notebooks for the boys.

'Why not just throw money at them?' Jack sneered.

Antonia lifted her head and glared at him.

'Why am I the enemy of the people again?' she spat back. 'What's with you, Jack? I've bought fresh food for us all.'

She looked at the bundles lying in the hot sun.

'We'd better get the fish on board.'

'Leave it!' Jack snapped. 'Get down below!'

'We'd been getting on so well,' Antonia murmured as she slipped down the ladder.

She gave a shriek as Curly's head popped up from a hole in the floor. She hadn't even noticed that the boards of the cabin were up when she'd rushed down below earlier.

'Mining for gold?' she quipped.

Then she saw that Curly's face was as set and as grim as Jack's. He didn't look a bit like her friend and supporter any more. He swung out of the hole and stood silently next to Jack. Antonia sat down at the table and looked directly at the two men.

'OK, what have I done?'

Jack placed some twisted wires, a few copper screws, a broken alarm clock and a glass bulb full of liquid on the table before her.

'Oh, it's that kids' television programme!' she joked. 'You give me two empty toilet rolls and a washing-up bottle and I make a nuclear power reactor.'

She felt a twist in the pit of her stomach. Her subconscious mind had recognised the truth before she had. She stared silently at the bits on the table before her for a few moments longer, and then she raised her eyes to meet Jack's angry stare.

'It's a bomb, isn't it, put on board when we were away?'

There was no softening in his body language or in his eyes.

'And you're surprised?' he spat out.

Antonia shook her head and felt dizzy.

'I shouldn't be?'

Jack's voice was grim.

'You're a good little actress, but I think it's time for the truth now.'

'I feel like I'm trying to watch a movie starting in the middle,' Antonia said, putting her head in her hands. 'I can understand that you're not entirely happy that someone tried to blow up the Kingfisher, but why are you so mad at me?'

The flat of Jack's hand hit the table

with a tremendous slap. Bits of the home-made bomb rattled on the wood.

'Tell me the truth!' he bellowed.

'It'll go off!' Antonia screamed, staring at the contraption in horror.

Jack's teeth were clenched and so were his fists. His eyes blazed.

'I'm going to kill you in a minute!'

Antonia yelled right back at him, 'Why?'

Curly raised his hands and made motions of keeping them apart.

'Let's cool it now, folks,' he suggested. 'Antonia, is there anything about your brother we should maybe know?'

'The penny drops!' she said, banging her forehead. 'You think Max is a secret agent and the baddies are after him? Oh, please!'

'You were expecting trouble,' he said quietly.

'There's no big secret, I promise you.'

Jack shook his head.

'Why did you suspect the shop-keeper?'

'I just had a feeling, that's all.'

'I'm supposed to believe that you are Little Miss Innocent and trust your woman's intuition?'

'Take it easy,' Curly murmured. 'There is a sixth sense. All sailors know that.'

Jack folded his arms and glared down his nose at Antonia.

'Did you or did you not tell us the truth about your brother?'

Antonia met his angry gaze.

'My brother is a perfectly respectable anthropologist, nothing else.'

'No, he's not,' Jack said, gesturing towards the bomb. 'We mentioned his name, once, casually, and look what happened.'

'Whoa now!' Curly cut in. 'Jack, suppose Max lied to Antonia.'

Jack's head whipped towards his friend and then back to Antonia. He looked relieved.

'Of course! Could it be that the

mysterious Mr Max didn't tell his baby sister the truth about his trips.'

Antonia was fired up now.

'Don't be stupid! Max is so rich he could buy a university! What motive could he have?'

Jack shrugged.

'I admire your loyalty, baby, but some men just go bad.'

'Not Max,' she replied stubbornly.

Jack's eyes roamed over her face, examining every inch of her. He seemed to come to a decision.

'I believe you,' he announced. 'But I don't know your brother and until I can form my own judgement, we'd better assume he means big trouble.'

Curly was nodding his dark head.

'Antonia's in the clear,' he agreed. 'But Max could be one heavy dude.'

Jack stirred the bomb bits on the table with a thoughtful hand.

'All we had to do was turn on the gas, and blooey! No-one would have suspected a thing.'

Antonia felt her mouth drop.

'Excuse me? We all get blown to kingdom come and everyone leaves it at that?'

'Happens all the time,' Jack said. 'Number one killer at sea. Novices leave the gas on, it builds up under the deck, and then one little spark . . . '

Antonia felt a cold shiver up her spine. She looked up at Jack.

'What if they try again?'

Jack's eyes blazed with derision.

'We won't be here.'

'Amen to that,' Curly muttered, heading for the ladder.

As soon as he was up on deck, he let out a great shout.

'Jack!'

Jack went up the ladder so fast he hardly touched the rungs. Antonia scooted up behind him. The two men were looking out over the ocean. Very white on the blue horizon was a motor yacht, sleek, powerful, three storeys high, bristling with satellite dishes and slender antenna. She was moving fast. Antonia could already hear the steady rumble of the massive engines.

'Is it the marines to the rescue, or is it Mr Big?' Jack murmured thoughtfully.

Curly shrugged.

'No chance of outrunning that thing. We'll just have to wait and see.'

Antonia felt too apprehensive to stand on deck watching the big yacht power towards them.

'I'll cook dinner while we're waiting,' she announced brightly. 'My fish are probably fried already, leaving them on that hot jetty.'

Jack's eyes expressed admiration for her attitude. He gave her shoulder an approving squeeze.

'I'll help you stow the food,' he said softly.

'And I'll stay on watch,' Curly growled.

★   ★   ★

'I think I've died and gone to heaven,' Curly said, a few hours later, as he looked at the meal Antonia had produced for them.

'I'll second that,' Jack said reverently, inhaling deeply. 'I've got a bottle of wine I've been saving for a special occasion.'

He took a second look at the feast Antonia had spread out on a folding table on the deck.

'And this sure is special.'

He vanished below and came back with a bottle of Australian wine. He poured them each a glass.

'To Antonia, the best cook in the world.'

Antonia smiled. It was nice to think that after a week of being the girl who knew nothing she'd finally impressed the two men with something.

'Lobster bisque to start with,' she said, ladling it out. 'I used coconut cream because there's no dairy products. What do you think?'

'Blissful,' Jack said and Curly rolled his eyes.

'So your nanny did teach you to cook.'

Antonia laughed.

'Nanny could only make rice pudding! But she had lots of au-pairs to
help her. Celeste, who was French,
taught me the most.'

She took a mouthful of the soup.
Boastful or not, she had to admit it was
delicious. She gave Jack a cheeky grin.

'Better than noodles?'

'I'll say,' he agreed.

Afterwards, Jack insisted on clearing
the dishes away for her, and then he sat
watching her with an air of mixed
wonder and expectation as she brought
out the next course.

'Fried fish, sweet-potato chips, and
vegetables tossed in my secret dressing,'
Antonia said. 'How you boys can live
without vegetables is beyond me.'

'I never want to again.' Jack sighed.

He took a mouthful of the food and
rolled his eyes in total bliss.

'Antonia, will you teach me to cook?'

'Sure,' she said quickly, pleased that
he'd asked her. 'It's not hard. How
come you never tried it before?'

Jack shrugged, but Antonia saw pain in his eyes as he answered.

'We weren't allowed in the canteen at the home when I was small and my foster parents took food out of the freezer and put it into the microwave. After that I was busy getting through law school.'

'I'll make the coffee,' Jack volunteered.

'Don't you want pudding?' Antonia teased. 'There's a pineapple sponge in the oven.'

The appreciation she could see on Jack's face made all the trouble she'd taken worth while. She'd spent hours in the market, lingering over the exotic fruit and vegetables, bantering with the stallholders, asking their advice. Many of the islanders spoke a heavy patois that was a little difficult to understand, but she'd found them all friendly and helpful.

In fact, they'd given her so much advice that her head buzzed! As well as an array of fruit and vegetables, Antonia had bought yeast, flour and rice, pasta, corn and beans. One stallholder had reminded her she'd need oil, another had lined up the children to carry her bundles, and yet another had sold her the tablecloth that now adorned the table they were sitting around.

Antonia looked up from the table and smoothed the floaty dress she'd donned for the occasion. She took a sip of wine. She could feel the rise and fall of the yacht, caused by the tiny waves lapping under the Kingfisher. She could taste salt in the air — and the first good meal she'd had for weeks.

The sun was setting in streaks of red on the horizon and the sky was a deep, pale lavender above it. One bright star twinkled next to a crescent moon. She'd never been so happy. Jack put his spoon down with a contented sigh and rubbed his stomach.

'That hit the spot,' he remarked, and then his hazel eyes turned watchful. 'Oh, oh, here we go.'

All through the meal Antonia had

been conscious of the motor boat. It hadn't come in to the jetty, but had moored out in the middle of the bay. Close up, she was as big as an ocean liner. The front of the boat was pointing towards them, so they couldn't see the back, where the people were probably sitting. It was creepy, not knowing who was aboard her.

All the windows were of smoked glass. So far, they'd seen no-one. But now a small white dingy with a very big shiny engine on the back was buzzing towards them. The sound of the engine echoed around the quiet bay. Antonia surreptitiously reached for her handbag, but Jack's hand clamped on her wrist.

'You watch too many movies,' he told her. 'And besides, that gun isn't big enough to do more than annoy a gnat.'

'I wanted my lipstick,' she lied.

The look in Jack's brown eyes told her that he wasn't fooled for a minute, but he let go her wrist and fixed his attention on the approaching boat.

Antonia did freshen her lipstick and combed out her hair. Her hands shook slightly. Reflected in the tiny mirror she was using, she could see her mouth trembling. She was glad Jack and Curly were sitting next to her. As the engine died, silence fell over the bay. Jack and Curly said nothing. Antonia clenched her fists and waited.

'Ahoy, there!'

A short, round man with a red face was looking up at them from the dingy.

'Is your radio broken? I couldn't raise you at all.'

Jack blinked, then uncoiled himself and went to stand by the rail of the Kingfisher, looking down at the man.

'We only use it for the daily weather forecast, mate. It runs down the battery.'

The man laughed.

'I couldn't live without electricity. I bet you'd appreciate a gin and tonic with ice cubes.'

Antonia felt her mouth water. She

hadn't had a drink with ice in it since she'd got off the plane. She bobbed up from her seat.

'You have ice?'

She decided that the man had rather a sweet smile. It reached his eyes and lifted his round face nicely.

'My wife and daughter sent me to fetch some new company. They're getting tired of me.'

Antonia looked at Jack. Jack looked at Curly. Then all three of them nodded. Jack shouted down to the man.

'We've a few chores, yet. We'll be over in about fifteen minutes, if that's all right.'

The man grinned, fired up his engine, and went off with a wave.

'He seems all right, but let's be careful, man,' Curly said.

Jack nodded. Then he turned to Antonia.

'You put that dish down! We're washing up.'

'I'll get changed then,' she replied.

Jack's eyes were puzzled.

'Changed? You look like a princess already.'

'It's not a cocktail dress.'

Jack rolled his eyes up to the ceiling.

'Oh, Curly, what shall I wear tonight?'

His friend studied him gravely.

'You always look nice in sequins.'

Antonia glared at them both.

'Nanny always said that dressing properly shows respect to the host.'

Jack gave her a grim smile.

'What would she say about the correct wear for three little flies that might be stepping into the spider's parlour?'

Antonia clutched her stomach. She couldn't feel any butterflies there.

'They're probably OK,' she told him.

'Well, let's be careful until we're sure,' Jack told her.

★ ★ ★

'Fish, fish, fish, that's all Father thinks about,' Mrs Morrison whined.

125

Her daughter nodded sulkily.

'He won't take us anywhere nice.'

Antonia looked at the tropical paradise around them and smothered a smile.

'Where would you like to go?' she asked sympathetically.

'Somewhere with shops,' Donna Morrison answered.

'That I can relate to!' Antonia said. 'I went to the cutest little market today.'

'You went on shore?' Donna gasped.

'It's full of germs,' her mother said, shuddering. 'You wouldn't get me in one of those dirty places if you dragged me. Oh, Donna, if only your father had had the consideration to take us to Montego Bay.'

As Mrs Morrison continued to moan about the shortcomings of her husband, Antonia swished her drink so that the ice cubes tinkled in the cold glass. To think she'd looked forward to some girl talk! The men seemed to be having more fun. Mr Morrison was holding his hands out to show Jack and Curly the size of the fish he'd nearly caught. She smiled. Jack was clearly telling Mr Morrison what he should do next time. Curly threw in a comment that made all three men laugh. She wished she could join them. Mrs Morrison touched her arm.

'I asked you what part of London you came from, dear.'

'Kensington,' Antonia said. 'I live on Church Street.'

'You perhaps don't know the Bakers? They live nearby but, of course, they're rather exclusive.'

'I don't know them,' Antonia replied, 'but it's still a small world. Your friends must have rented the house from my aunt.'

'No!' Mrs Morrison exclaimed, her eyes glowing with excitement. 'Wait until I tell Susan Baker! Lady Stone-hill's niece on our yacht.'

She leaned forward confidentially.

'My dear, now that I know who you are, I couldn't think of you spending another moment with those rough, horrid men. You must join us.'

'Thank you, but we're sort of used to each other now,' Antonia said, trying to be diplomatic.

'No servants, no electricity, no facilities.'

Mrs Morrison lowered her voice.

'And no chaperone! You'll be much safer with us.'

'The boys take very good care of me,' Antonia replied, trying to imagine Mrs Morrison dismantling a bomb.

Mrs Morrison stared at her.

'I can't understand you,' she moaned. 'I don't know what Susan Baker will say if she hears I let Lady Stonehill's niece go off with those men. Maybe I should ring her.'

'Do you have a phone?' Antonia asked, brightening at once. 'I left mine in Swimp Island because there's nowhere to charge the batteries. I'd love to ring Daddy.'

'Ring anyone you like,' Mrs Morrison said hospitably. 'I won't feel as if I'm abandoning you if people know where you are. We've only got one mobile but you can use the phone on the bridge. The captain will show you how.'

* * *

Jack leaned back in his well-upholstered sun-lounger and grinned at the girl opposite him. Her mother might have written him off as socially negligible, but Donna Morrison clearly found him interesting. She was flirting for all she was worth, which was agreeable enough in itself, but he was finding that sulky, rich girls did nothing for him.

He liked them trim and sassy, like Antonia, who was walking back from the bridge, looking like a million dollars in her black cocktail dress. Then he noticed that her eyes were troubled. They looked cloudy and sad. Jack got up from his seat, leaving Donna in the middle of a long story about trying to match nail polish, and went to Antonia.

She was standing by the rail, looking

out to sea. Fairy lights strung around the motor yacht made him feel as if he were at a party, and soft music played from hidden loudspeakers, heightening the luxurious effect.

'Did you get through to your father?' he asked.

Antonia turned to face him. He could see hurt in the blue eyes.

'He wasn't very pleased with me. It's four o'clock in the morning in England.'

'What did he say?' Jack asked.

'He's got a new gamekeeper and he thinks that the new pheasant feeders are working out better than the old ones.'

Jack wanted to put his arms around her when he heard the quiver in her voice, but he knew that he had to stay focused.

'Anything about Max?'

Antonia's dark lashes swept down and then up. She sniffed before answering.

'Maybe I didn't explain properly, but

he seemed to think I was making it all up.'

'It does sound a bit fantastic,' Jack agreed.

Inside he was bursting with sympathy for Antonia. Her brother could be in danger. She was on her own on the other side of the world with two strange men, and her father didn't seem to care. He wished he could make things better for her. Antonia looked up at him. He could tell she was forcing a smile.

'Daddy said things will probably turn out OK. He's usually right.'

Jack met the sweet honesty of her gaze.

'He'll be right,' he declared.

Antonia heard the promise in his voice and looked at him, solemnly, directly. He looked at her for a moment longer. He wanted to tell her how he felt, how she made him feel, but he couldn't find the words.

'More drinks, anybody?' Donna Morrison trilled, barging between them.

'I've got a special Polish vodka,' she purred, fluttering her eyelashes. 'Just the thing for a strong sailor like you.'

Jack caught Antonia rolling her eyes. He felt a smile inside. She was looking at Donna's face with a wearied expression. Then his smile turned into a frown. He'd only known her a few days. He couldn't possibly know what she was thinking. Antonia's eyes might hold disdain for Donna Morrison but her words were polite.

'No more drinks for us, thank you, Donna. We're setting off early in the morning, aren't we, Jack?'

Could Antonia be hurrying him away because she was jealous? Jack liked that idea, but then he realised that she must be thinking about finding Max.

'That's right. We're sailing to Sugar Cay, first thing,' he agreed, carefully watching the Morrisons as he spoke.

He was pleased to see no reaction. As they said their good-nights and got in the Kingfisher's dinghy, he decided that the family on the motor yacht were exactly what they seemed to be. Jack dipped the oars into the dark glass of the tropical water. Stars spangled the velvet sky that hung over the bay. The music from the Morrisons' yacht floated nostalgically over the water towards them as they rowed home. Antonia, he noticed, seemed to be deep in thought.

7

Antonia kept watch as they approached Sugar Cay on the other side from the only village on the island. It seemed to be deserted. Nobody hailed them as they turned and sailed along the coastline. The cliffs were so overgrown with greenery that they looked like moss-covered castles.

They looked impassable, but Jack turned the boat into a deep, sheltered inlet and moored the Kingfisher next to a tiny opening in the cliff side. Through the gap in the rocks, Antonia could see coconut palms.

'The boat looks very white,' Antonia said, looking at the yacht critically.

'Couldn't we camouflage her with some dead coconut fronds?'

'Good thinking,' Jack said.

He scrambled off the boat and passed armfuls of vegetation to her.

'Jack,' she said as she worked in the hot sun, 'what if Max isn't there?'

His eyes were very kind.

'Then we'll look for him somewhere else.'

She felt some of the worry lift off her shoulders.

'There,' he said, stepping back and looking at the boat critically. 'Now we'll have something to eat, and then Curly sets off to explore.'

Antonia frowned.

'I still think I should go with him.'

'You'd never pass for an islander in that classy little number.'

'Do you like it?' Antonia said, feeling pleased as she smoothed down the pleated skirt. 'I wasn't sure about orange.'

'Bright colours suit you,' Jack told her, and his eyes told her even more.

Antonia turned away and pretended to be busy getting lunch. As she wrapped a home-made pasty in foil for Curly to take with him, she wondered what it would be like to be alone with

Jack. It was going to be strange without her chaperone.

As soon as they'd eaten, Curly set off, slipping away into the palm trees with hardly a sound, keeping out of sight as much as possible. Antonia and Jack then set off to explore the area around the boat.

Antonia scrambled over a pile of boulders, feeling glad that she'd invested in some flat sandals from the market on Galliwasp.

'Could there be any danger?' she asked anxiously.

Jack glanced at her. His eyes were sombre.

'We should be OK near the boat, but after that bomb, I'm taking no chances.'

Antonia fell silent. Suddenly she understood her father's reaction. She'd seen the device with her own eyes, and she didn't believe it, or at least, she couldn't believe the bomb was anything to do with Max. As they walked on, Antonia was convinced that Curly would find her brother living in the main village, happily absorbed in his studies.

She pictured Max explaining how his birthday message must have gone astray, and laughing about her ridiculous suspicions. She paused and brushed her damp hair off her forehead. Then Max would go back to work and she'd go back to London, which sounded like a great idea.

'Jack, I'm so hot. Can I have a drink, please?'

He stopped, and she scrambled to catch up with him and then looked up at his stern face.

'What are we looking for?' she moaned.

'Don't know,' he replied, passing her the water bottle. 'Just checking the lie of the land.'

'It's hot, green and jungly,' Antonia grumbled, lifting the bottle to her lips. 'What else do you need to know?'

'Bear up,' Jack said, smiling at her. 'This is as far as I want to go. We'll work our way back in a semi-circle towards the boat.'

The air seemed to grow even hotter as they walked, and then Antonia heard the cooling rush of water. Golden shafts of sunlight pierced the green, and the forest opened out into a glade. On the far side, a stream tumbled over a rocky river bed and fell in a small waterfall into an emerald green pool of water.

'Orchids!' Antonia cried. 'I never knew they grew in trees!'

Jack's eyes were amused.

'Did you think their natural habitat was the florist's shop?'

Antonia gazed at him haughtily.

'Go on then, Mr Natural History expert. What kind of butterflies are flitting across the glade? And I want the Latin names, please.'

He threw up his hands, laughing.

'You win. And before you ask, those dragonflies zooming over the water are red, and that's all I can tell you.'

Antonia sat on one of the boulders at the side of the pool. She splashed cold water over her face, neck and arms. It felt luxurious on her hot flesh. She turned her head to look at Jack. He was watching the crystal drops roll down her skin with an intentness that made her nervous.

Her throat was tight as she asked him, 'Can we swim?'

'Sure. It looks safe enough. Do you have the right coloured bathers to hand?'

'Cheeky!' Antonia said, flipping her orange dress over her head.

Jack blinked when he saw her in nothing but a bright orange swimsuit, but he said nothing, and took off his own shirt and shorts to reveal neat black trunks.

'Last one in's a dead possum,' he called.

Screaming with pleasure, Antonia rushed into the cool opal pool. The water enveloped her in a caress that was both sensual and soothing as it lapped around her sun-warmed skin. She dived under the water, rolled over like a porpoise, and then burst to the surface feeling magnificent.

She swam alongside Jack without speaking. Words seemed unnecessary to communicate such simple pleasures. At first just playing with the water was enough, but gradually, naturally, inevitably, they swam closer and closer together, until finally they were standing together in the shadows to one side of the waterfall.

Antonia looked into the clear hazel of Jack's eyes and knew that he was going to kiss her. She lifted her bare arms and wound them around his neck, encouraging him. His lips touched hers, thrilling her and claiming her as his. Antonia felt gorgeous exhilaration streak around her body. She felt young and joyfully innocent as she returned his kiss. Jack pulled away and looked at her with wonder clear in his eyes. He was smiling. Antonia looked back at him and laughed for the sheer joy of being alive.

'Your eyes look like amber in this light,' she told him. 'I used to think they were brown, but they're not, are they?'

Jack's hands slid up and held her chin. He kissed her eyes, her cheeks, her mouth. And then he sighed deeply.

'We have to get back.'

Antonia lifted her head and claimed one more kiss, and then she, too, sighed in her turn.

'I'll carry my dress until I'm dry.'

They held hands as they walked back to the Kingfisher, stopping every now and then to embrace once again.

'The smell of coconuts will always make me think of you,' Antonia promised, as they walked dreamily through the plantation towards the gap in the cliffs.

The Kingfisher was silent and deserted. Antonia felt the magic of her mood leaking away. The first faint flutter began in her stomach.

'Shouldn't Curly be back?'

'An hour ago,' Jack said tersely. 'Did we eat all your fresh bread for breakfast?'

'I saved some for sandwiches.'

Jack made them both sandwiches. He ate some of his on the boat, but Antonia saw with misgiving that he was wrapping the rest to take with him. She kept quiet as he added water, a map and a rope to his growing pile, but she had to protest when she saw him roll up a sleeping bag.

'You're not going to stay out all night?'

Jack flashed her a quick look.

'Have you seen my torch?'

'I'm coming with you.'

He stopped packing and met her eyes directly.

'You wait here.'

'I could help you,' she said assuredly.

Jack shook his head firmly.

'It might be dangerous.'

He was so stubborn that Antonia wanted to shake him.

'So you'll need help even more.'

He was glaring at her now, standing close.

'I'll tie you to the mast if you don't stop arguing.'

Antonia looked at the set stubbornness of his chin and heaved a great sigh.

'The male ego is so boring.'

She sat on the bench seat that ran around the cabin table and put her chin on her hands. Jack looked relieved.

'I know it's hard to wait,' he told her kindly as he slung a full rucksack on his back. 'I should be back in an hour.'

'And if you're not?'

He looked solemn.

'You remember how to send an emergency distress signal?'

Antonia smiled.

'You made me practise it every day.'

Jack nodded. He hesitated before stepping over the side of the Kingfisher and on to dry land. His eyes told Antonia how much he wanted to say.

'Go on!' she said, flipping a hand at him.

He gave her a quick grin and turned to walk through the plantation, moving even more silently than Curly had done. The boat felt very quiet and empty. Antonia had never been alone on the Kingfisher before. Nervously, she checked the radio. She remembered Jack's drills perfectly, but they'd both forgotten one fact. They were moored inside a high, rocky inlet, and the cliffs were blocking the radio signal. She fiddled uselessly with the dead radio for a few minutes and then chewed her bottom lip while she came to a decision.

First she changed her dress for a dull-green ensemble, then she tied a matching silk scarf over her hair. Finally she opened her handbag and took out her gun. There was spare ammunition in her suitcase, so, feeling rather theatrical, she dropped the whole box of bullets into her pocket.

She didn't know what use the gun would be. Despite her country upbringing, Antonia had been far too soft-hearted to shoot at any living target, so her experience was limited to clay pigeon shooting.

'But I was a whiz at that!' she reminded herself.

It didn't help her to feel much braver. She hesitated, and decided to wait a little longer. She sat on the back of the boat, straining her eyes over the empty plantation, but saw nothing. As the hot afternoon wore away the butterflies in her stomach made her feel so jittery that she knew she'd have to go. She waited for one long, last minute, but there was no sign of Jack or Curly returning.

Antonia slipped over the side of the boat, put on her flat sandals, and set off along the trail through the plantation.

★   ★   ★

Curly scratched his skin vigorously.

'Bugs!' he muttered.

A tall man, who would have been good-looking save for the ragged, auburn beard that stuck out from his chin, turned to look at Curly sympathetically. The blue eyes above his sharp cheek bones held the dreamy, abstract air of the academic.

145

'I'm afraid that our little prison is seen as the promised land by a host of assorted parasites.'

'Never mind,' Curly said firmly.

He gingerly arranged a smelly blanket on a broken-off door balanced on two packing crates and lay down on it.

'Jack will get us out.'

A few seconds later the door opened and two men moving with remarkable efficiency tossed a man-sized bundle on to the floor of the hut. The door shut. The sacking bundle moved, groaned, and out popped the head of a man with brown hair. The academic-looking man with a beard turned to Curly and lifted an eyebrow.

'One presumes that this will be Jack.'

'What?' the bundle groaned. 'Get this sack off me.'

When he was free, Jack sat up and looked around him. He was in a hot, dark, airless hut made of corrugated iron. It had no window. There were no chairs. People sat on a dirty floor of packed earth. A wax night-light flickered in a saucer, lighting up Curly's remorseful face.

'Sorry, Jack,' he said.

'Me, too,' Jack said briefly, looking around at the other people in the hut, locking eyes with the thin, clever-looking man first.

'You have to be Antonia's brother!'

Max nodded gravely before he spoke.

'Let me introduce you to your fellow countryman, Steve Jones, who was unfortunate enough to call here as part of his round-the-world sailing trip.'

A scrawny, fair-haired youngster nodded at Jack.

'G'day.'

Max continued, 'And this is Mavis Marley, who was swept away from her holiday group while scuba-diving.'

Mavis gave Jack a sweet, shy smile, but her dark eyes were on Curly as she spoke.

'I suppose I'm lucky to be alive. The current swept me for miles. But of all the beaches in all the world, I had to land on this one.'

Curly bent over her in a protective manner.

'We'll get you out of this,' he promised.

Then he turned to Jack. There was no mistaking the pride in his voice.

'Mavis is professor of Mediaeval Literature at London University.'

'Ah,' Jack said, watching Mavis return Curly's adoring look with one of her own. 'Who's going to tell me what else is going on around here?'

'A drug factory,' Max said succinctly.

Jack blinked.

'But poppies don't grow in the Caribbean.'

The academic gave him a dry smile.

'All the more reason not to look for a plant that processes them. As I understand it, these people set up an operation on a deserted island, ship the stuff in raw, pay the locals handsomely to process it, and then move out within a year, before anyone can catch up with them.'

Jack looked at Max.

'How long have you been here?'

'Ever since I landed, four months ago. They've been making use of us castaways as free labour, although my feeling is that the gang is about ready to wind up their operations here.'

Jack had to know the worst.

'And when they leave?'

Max's eyes were shadowed.

'They've said that they'll leave us behind.'

Mavis said quickly, 'We're no threat to them. By the time we could raise the alarm, they'll be long gone.'

'I expect you're right,' Max said aloud, but his eyes told Jack that privately he held a different view.

'We have to get out,' Jack said.

Max shrugged.

'They watch us constantly, and where would you go?'

'The Kingfisher, my boat. She's moored in a rocky inlet not very far away.'

Max shook his head.

'They'll have found your vessel and

149

scuttled her by now.'

Jack felt fear clutch at his heart.

'Antonia's on board. I told her to radio for help if I wasn't back in an hour.'

'I know that inlet,' Max said. 'Your radio won't work. No signal.'

'How could I have forgotten? Of all the stupid fools!'

Max put out a hand. His eyes were curious, and understanding, as they measured the depth of Jack's emotions.

'Take it easy,' he said gently. 'They won't hurt Antonia.'

Curly lifted his dark head.

'Maybe you underestimate her.'

Max looked incredulous.

'My little sister? She knows nothing about real life.'

'She's pretty resourceful,' Jack said slowly. 'And maybe they won't find the boat, at least not tonight. Antonia camouflaged it.'

Max's tone was unconvinced.

'She'd call her therapist if she broke a nail.'

The night-light flickered and filled the air with the smell of hot wax.

'We only get one light,' Max said. 'Folks, we need to make a bed for Jack.'

Curly and Mavis seemed more than happy to share a narrow bunk, leaving the foul-smelling blanket and the hard door to Jack. He lay on his back, looking up at the dusty, corrugated-iron ceiling, waiting for the door to open and Antonia to fly in.

Nothing happened.

After about an hour, Jack could tell from Steve Jones' breathing that the young Australian had gone to sleep.

'Max?' he said quietly.

Antonia's brother was awake.

'She'll be all right.'

Jack leaned up on one elbow.

'We should be ready.'

Max laughed derisively.

'In case my baby sister comes storming to the rescue?'

Curly's deep voice filled the hut.

'Mavis and I are staying ready.'

Jack was thankful for his friend's

loyal support. He lay down, feeling better. Silence fell inside the hut. The air was hot and sticky. It was impossible to sleep. Jack tried to fight off the suffocating fear he felt and then tried to kid himself that he'd be just as worried about any of his party who was missing, but it was no good. Antonia's face filled his mind, and he knew that he was capable of killing any man who touched her.

A mosquito whined across the hot air and bit him. Jack slapped at it viciously. The low-pitched whine was so annoying. He supposed he was lucky there was only one. He turned over yet again. And then he sat bolt upright.

Gunfire!

'Wake up!' he snapped.

Curly was by his side in an instant. The others woke up more slowly. Outside there was more gunfire and yells, shouts and a scream, followed by so many explosions that it sounded like a fireworks factory exploding.

'Jack?' a low voice by the door called.

'Antonia!'

He wanted to strangle her for putting herself in danger, and then he wanted to laugh out loud and shout to the world that there had never been a woman as unbelievable, as courageous, as beautiful, as surprising and as gutsy as Antonia. He heard metal scraping on corrugated iron, and then the door swung open. He wanted to reach out and take her slim body in his arms and bury his face in her hair, but she was whispering urgently.

'Come on! The bullets will be all gone in a moment. I threw them on the fire.'

Curly, Mavis and Steve Jones slipped out into the dark, followed by Max. So many tropical stars blazed in the sky, that it seemed quite light compared to the darkness of the hut. Jack could see the radiant expression on Antonia's face. She reached out and briefly touched one of her brother's hands, but all she said was, 'Max! Hurry up!'

They ran across the clearing, heading

for the safety and concealment of the jungle. First Mavis, then Curly, then the young Australian reached the undergrowth. Max's long, lean figure followed them into the greenery and vanished.

Jack turned around to say jubilantly, 'We've done it!'

And then he saw the man who was chasing Antonia. Tall, scruffy and unshaven, the man's well-built body was clad in ripped army fatigues. He was holding a gun. For a frozen instant of panic, Jack thought he was going to use it, but then he saw that the man had other ideas. There was no mistaking the expression on his face.

The man's long legs took him closer to Antonia. He punched her in the small of the back, knocking her off balance. She stumbled and, unable to check her headlong pace, fell to the ground. The man slung his gun over one shoulder and leaned over her. He took a coil of thin rope from his pocket. Without stopping to look around for a weapon, Jack launched himself at Antonia's attacker.

Antonia had hit the ground so hard that she felt sick and dizzy. She knew it was important that she get up and run, but a mysterious force seemed to be holding her down. It was all she could do to breathe. And then she smelled rum and stale sweat and became aware of a face from a thousand nightmares bending over her. She wanted to scream, but the scream got caught up in her empty airways and made it even harder to breathe.

As if he knew how to hurt her most, her attacker caught her around the neck and his arm crushed her throat. Still half-lying on the ground, Antonia's hands came up to claw at the man's arm. His forearm was as strong as a metal pipe. Her nails slipped off the slackness of his skin without leaving a mark.

Then she heard a dull thud, and the grip on her throat loosened and her attacker fell sideways. For one blinding flash, her eyes locked with Jack's, and then he turned away and dropped into a fighting crouch, ready to take the man on. A burst of warmth, love and gladness exploded in her heart. Jack had come for her! Then she became aware that the sound of gunfire had stopped. Her bullets must have burned up. She could hear confused shouting in the camp, but soon they would discover that they were not under attack and begin to restore order.

The breath of life was rushing into her now. She rolled over on the ground and stood up. Jack was still facing her attacker, but she saw the man's arm reach behind him and the realisation that he was reaching for his gun entered her heart like an arrow. Jack seemed to see the gun at the same moment, because he launched himself at the man and held on to his arm, preventing him from reaching for his weapon.

Close up, the attacker looked twice as large as Jack. Antonia looked around her for a weapon. Her breath was coming in panicky gasps and her hands shook as she rummaged around the edge of the jungle, running a few steps one way and then a few steps the other way, looking for a weapon.

A trailing green frond — that was no good. A bush with thick branches, but they were too thick to pull off. It was no good. She couldn't find anything. And then a hand grabbed her arm and pushed a knobbly branch in it.

'Here!' a familiar voice said, and she saw Max's eyes flash in the starlight.

He was holding a branch just like the one he'd given her, and was advancing on Jack and the attacker, who were now rolling on the ground. Antonia ran after him. Max moved towards the heads of the two struggling men. He seemed to be waiting for a chance to hit the aggressor over the head, but the two men were rolling over and over as they fought, and it was difficult to pick a moment.

Antonia stood by the side of the two struggling men, waited until the ample target made by the buttocks of the man who had knocked her down was waving in the air, and swung her branch down hard. He gave a great shout, sat up, and turned towards her, fury in his black eyes. Max seized the opportunity and swung his branch down hard on the man's head. Antonia saw the whites of his eyes as he passed out. Jack scrambled to his feet.

'Run!' he said urgently. 'They'll be here any minute.'

Antonia could hear shouting coming from the camp area. She turned at once and ran for the jungle, Max and Jack behind her. They were into the first concealing layer of undergrowth. Every step made their escape more secure, but they kept running.

'More to the left,' Jack hissed.

Antonia had lost her sense of direction, but she followed him obediently. They ran for another five minutes, then Jack said, 'Slow down and move quietly.'

Shadows rustled around them. As

they walked quietly, the tropical frogs started up their night chorus, and Antonia realised how wise Jack had been. Now the jungle sounds were back to normal, no-one could track them down in the dark — she hoped.

By the time they got to the coconut plantation near the cliffs, her legs were shaking with fatigue. Jack slipped a supportive arm under her elbow and eased her on to a rock.

'Wait here and rest. I'm going to see if the gang found the Kingfisher.'

Antonia sat next to Max, holding his hand, trying not to think about what they would do if the boat wasn't there. A breeze blew off the sea, cooling her hot, dampened face, but it made the dry palm fronds above her click and scrape together in such a spooky manner that she wanted to scream.

Where were Curly and Mavis? And the Australian boy?

Jack suddenly appeared out of the darkness. His eyes seemed to catch the overhead starlight and reflect it back.

'They didn't find her!' he whispered jubilantly. 'Come on.'

'What about Curly?' Antonia asked.

She saw his brow furrow.

'I don't know. We'll get the boat ready to go to sea, then we'll decide.'

Then they heard a twig crack on the other side of the plantation. Oh, no, Antonia thought, please, don't let it be those men.

Jack gripped her arm tight, but then she felt all his muscles relax and he pointed to three dark shadows, one very much larger than the other two. The smallest shadow was limping.

'It's the others!' His voice was joyful. 'Let's get the sails up and get out of here!'

8

Antonia was sitting on the white beach of Swimp Island surrounded by children when she became aware of Jack's soft footfalls moving over the sand towards her.

'Play it again,' Buddy's little brother begged, and his friends agreed. 'Sing the Ticky Ticky, Boom Boom song,' they pleaded.

Antonia smiled at the children who were clustered around her.

'You sing it,' she suggested, passing the doll she'd made out of a yam root to Buddy. 'I bet you can remember the words by now.'

'Boom!' he shouted, waving the doll and making the smaller children squeal in delight. 'Ticky Ticky Boom Boom is coming for you!'

The little ones scattered, running down the hot beach and plunging into the salty waves with screams of laughter. Antonia scrambled to her feet and put one hand to her forehead, protecting her eyes from the bright sun that shone in the blue, blue sky.

'Hello, Jack.'

His face was set in stone.

'Got a message for you.'

She wanted to shake him. Ever since they'd landed back on Swimp Island he'd been putting up walls, and she was on the other side. He'd been a little distant on the Kingfisher, but so had they all. After their dramatic experience, all five people had retreated into the privacy of their thoughts on the voyage home, as far as they could due to the vessels and helicopters of the police, coastguard and military that had swarmed around after Jack raised the alarm.

Antonia had thought she understood Jack. She, too, was scared by the depth of her love. It was scary to need another person. It was a big adjustment. So she'd given him space, thinking it was the right thing to do. But as soon as they landed on Swimp Island, she found out how wrong she'd been.

The first person they had seen was an elderly British gentleman with worried blue eyes under his battered hat. He was wearing crumpled old cricket flannels and looked uncomfortably hot. Next to him stood another elderly gentleman wearing what looked like a naval uniform from the Second World War.

'Daddy!' Antonia screamed, flinging herself into the arms of the man wearing the cricket outfit.

'Don't knock me over, Antonia,' he chided, but there was love in his eyes and he returned her hug with arms that shook a little.

'Daddy!' she chattered. 'Look! We found Max! And this is Curly.'

Curly stepped over and shook Mr Everett-Cox's hand.

That's quite a daughter you've got there, sir.'

'I'm beginning to realise that,' he

said, his eyes fixed on his daughter.

Then he looked up and saw his son. He gave a very British cough.

'Ah, Max.'

Max stepped forward and wrung his father's hand. Then he turned to Jack.

'This is Jack Bentley, owner and captain of the Kingfisher. We owe him so much.'

Antonia's father gripped Jack's hands.

'It seems that I owe you on behalf of both of my children. I don't know how to thank you.'

Jack's gaze fell away from the kindly blue eyes.

'It's nothing. She hired me to find him,' he muttered.

He extricated his hands and slouched away towards the hotel, leaving Antonia staring after him in dismay. Her father seemed unruffled by his brusqueness.

'Some people hate to be thanked,' he murmured.

Max was watching Antonia's face.

'This time it might be more complicated.'

Antonia felt as if she'd been slapped. Jack's emotional withdrawal had hurt more than any blow, but what could she do? No promises had passed between them; no words of love, only tender looks and intimate kisses. Yet she felt as if he'd broken a contract.

She approached Jack now as he stood on the hot white beach before her. Sadness filled her heart as she saw that his eyes were wary. His tone was cold and detached when he spoke.

'Your father's ready to leave.'

Antonia wanted to shout, 'Talk to me, Jack!' but instead she rose and fell into step beside him.

'Isn't Charles a darling? He hadn't spoken to Daddy for twenty years, but he came straight to the rescue,' she said.

'The Caribbean's full of men with no families and nothing to do,' Jack answered brutally.

White-hot anger flared through Antonia as she thought of all Jack was deliberately blocking out of his life.

She stopped, planted her hands on her hips and screamed at him, her voice as high and wild as the seagulls that swooped over the crashing surf.

'How do you think you're going to end up?'

His eyes stared into hers with an unfamiliar expression, for three long seconds that felt like a lifetime. And then his face twisted furiously and he turned away without speaking. Antonia could feel her heart beating as she watched him march away down the beach. She could see by the set of his shoulders that he was hurting, but there seemed to be no way to reach him. She took a last look at his familiar back, the way his thick hair curled over his collar, the strong brown legs under his shorts.

'Damn him!' she muttered furiously as she strode back to the hotel. 'Damn him! Damn him! Damn him!'

Because Swimp Island didn't have a jetty, Max, Curly, Mavis, Steve Jones, her father and Charles were gathered on the sandy beach, surrounded by piles of luggage.

'Here she is,' Max joked. 'It'll take at least three trips in your dinghy, Charles, before we get my sister's luggage out to your boat.'

'Not a problem,' Charles said.

'I'll take it!' Buddy offered, who was hanging around, like most of the islanders, watching the fun. 'You can hire my dinghy, Miss Antonia.'

Antonia swallowed a lump in her throat.'

'I won't need it, thank you, Buddy.'

Her father's eyes were astonished.

'You're staying here?'

Antonia nodded.

'I can catch the next steamer.'

Her father frowned.

'There's no saying when that will be.'

'I'm not in a hurry.'

He examined her face carefully.

'I'll miss you.'

She looked at him, surprised.

'You will?'

He nodded and kissed her forehead gently.

'Of course I'll miss you. I do love you, you know, Antonia, and I'm very proud of you.'

He cleared his throat.

'Have you got enough money?'

Antonia smiled at him lovingly.

'Heaps, thank you, Daddy. I'll be fine.'

'Do you know, my dear, I rather believe you will.'

' 'Course she will,' Curly said, letting go of Mavis's hand for just long enough to say goodbye to Antonia. 'Go get him, girl.'

Antonia hugged him back and then turned to Mavis.

'Invite me to your wedding,' she teased.

Antonia stayed on the beach until every last scrap of luggage had been ferried out to Charles's yacht. She sat in the shade of a palm tree that rustled in the ocean breeze. Buddy sat next to her on the white sand.

'Why are you crying?' he asked her.

Antonia touched her cheeks and

found they were wet.

'Charles's boat looks so beautiful under sail,' she answered vaguely.

Buddy looked out across the cobalt sea. The breeze was lifting the white sails of the yacht so that they looked like fabulous, curved wings.

'Jack's boat is even more beautiful,' he answered loyally. 'Are you going sailing in the Kingfisher again?'

She looked into his concerned little face and tried to hide her sadness, but it was hard to make her answer light.

'I don't know, Buddy. Maybe. It depends on Jack.'

★   ★   ★

Jack stood at the back of a circle of yelling, screaming, happy men, feeling quite cut off from them. He dug one foot into the coarse sand. He couldn't even remember which wrestler he'd put a bet on, let alone work up an interest in the results. Dogs barked, cockerels crowed, the bookies screamed the odds, it was all colour, movement and chaos. He took a drink of rum, but it lay heavily on his stomach. He just wasn't in the mood for this.

But he couldn't think what else to do, so he remained at the back of the outdoor wrestling ring, forcing himself to smile if he caught the eye of someone he knew, pretending to have a good time. He knew that Charles, the ex-navy man, would have set sail by now, taking advantage of the high tide that had turned half an hour ago and was flowing over the reef right now, taking all his friends on to Jamaica, where they'd get a flight home.

He felt an emptiness that was close to panic when he thought of them all leaving him. It's Curly I'll miss, he told himself. He tried to imagine his friend in London and shook his head in wonder. Who would have thought that such a confirmed bachelor would fall so hard and so quickly? And so easily! Curly made no bones about being madly in love with Mavis.

Jack felt worse than ever. He put a wad of local currency on one wrestler who was promptly knocked out in the first round.

'Just my luck,' Jack muttered.

He looked at the rapt faces around him and knew that things had changed for him. He no longer belonged. Maybe it was time to go home to Sydney and think about what to do next, or maybe he'd go to London. He didn't want to miss Curly's wedding, that was for sure.

Jack decided he'd go back to the hotel and take a nap. He turned away from the wrestling, and at that moment he saw Antonia. His heart exploded with pleasure before he could stop the emotional reaction. She looked so charming, standing amongst the islanders, like a bird of paradise in a flock of starlings.

Her hair was loose on her shoulders, and as usual she wore a bright colour, a flame-red dress, although he noticed that she'd left off her fashion shoes and was still wearing the flat sandals she'd bought at the market on Galliwasp.

She was so beautiful, and it wasn't just her fashion-plate exterior. He loved the generous heart and fighting spirit that he'd discovered she possessed. He'd known that he loved her ever since they'd kissed under the waterfall on Sugar Cay, but he'd been fighting the knowledge ever since. Life had taught him not to trust easily, and his heart told him that Antonia had the power to hurt him so badly he'd never recover. He wanted nothing of her. He glanced at her face, then looked quickly away from the sweet shyness in her eyes.

'Thought you'd gone,' he said gruffly.

Antonia smiled and moved a step nearer.

'There's unfinished business between us.'

Jack flipped a hand at her.

'Keep the money.'

Antonia's hand flew to her mouth.

'I'd forgotten! I owe you fifteen hundred dollars!'

'I don't want it,' Jack said, turning away.

He started to walk down the sandy path that led away from the village and down to the beach. Antonia followed behind him. He could smell her perfume and the sweet scent of her hair.

'Jack, you know I wasn't talking about money.'

Jack walked even faster.

'I hate clinging women,' he muttered. 'One kiss and they think they own you.'

'Don't you walk away from me, Jack Bentley!' she cried.

Jack stopped just short of the beach and turned around to look at her. He loved her courage, her sparkiness. He loved everything about her. So what stubborn instinct made him block out the truth and lie?

'I'm a loner.'

Antonia's eyes roamed over his face.

'No, you're not,' she said softly. 'You need me.'

'I don't.'

Her look was so steady that it was

difficult to meet it.

'You do! There's no Curly to sail with now.'

Jack turned and walked through the soft white sand and then down to the harder wet sand by the sea. He lifted his head and looked out over the blue. A tiny white dot was the Kingfisher, moored out in the deep water. He wished now he'd set sail in her this morning. That way he'd have been able to avoid this painful scene. He waded into the warm surf and started to walk along the edge of the sea. He could taste salt on his lips and seabirds cried overhead. Antonia followed behind him.

'I could be more than just a sailing partner,' she told him.

Despite her brave words, he could hear a quiver in her voice that touched his heart. One minute she was goading him until he exploded, the next he ached with the urge to take her in his arms and cherish her. But that was why she was dangerous. She touched his emotions in a way he didn't know how to handle. He didn't look at her.

'I'm all right!' he shouted back over his shoulder, continuing to wade through the surf.

He could hear her splashing along beside him, and then the splashing stopped. Had she given up at last and gone back to the hotel? Jack didn't want to look, but he slowed his pace somewhat.

'Jack.'

Antonia's voice was low, and he could hear a final note in it that warned him that he'd lose her if he didn't listen. He stopped and turned round to face her. His heart squeezed in his chest at the picture she made. She stood ankle deep in the fabulous Caribbean, a red splash in nature's blue palette.

Blue sky arched above her and blue sea spread out behind. The wind from the sea tossed her hair over her shoulders and he noticed that the sun had put a dusting of light freckles over her nose and a warm glow over her cheekbones.

He was afraid that if he looked up and met her honest gaze he'd be lost for ever. He kept his eyes trained on the perfect pink leaf of her mouth. It trembled slightly, and then opened and asked, 'Are you truly all right without me, Jack?'

It was his last chance and he knew it. The habits that he'd built up over a loveless childhood hampered him now. Lifelong caution and the feeling that it wasn't safe to hand out his heart warred with the desire to take Antonia in his arms and confess how much he loved her. He owed it to her to answer her question honestly.

Was he all right without her?

He stood in the hot sun listening to the ebb and flow of the waves about him. Antonia stood silent, watching him, seeming to know that he was examining his feelings. First came the surface answer. She'd upset him a bit, but he'd been perfectly all right before he'd met her, and he'd soon get back to normal. He licked his lips, tasting salt, and half turned his head to tell her to go away.

Then came the truth, crashing into his mind in a painful wave of memories. No, he wasn't all right. He hadn't been all right since the car crash that had taken his parents away when he was seven years old. He'd survived the children's home and the death of his foster mother, but surviving was a long way from being all right, and at some deep level he'd known that all along.

He'd tried to fill the hole in his heart where the love of a family should have been, first with money and success as a lawyer, and then by running away to a beachcomber's life in the Caribbean. But he hadn't been all right, not until he met Antonia. She was all that was good and bright in his life, and, yes, she could hurt him, but it was worth a chance. He turned back to look at her, and this time he met her gaze openly, with love.

'I hate shopping,' he told her, smiling.

A mischievous imp started to dance in the blue of her eyes.

'I'll take the kids.'

The idea terrified him, but it was strangely seductive as well.

'I don't know how to bring up a family,' he warned her.

Antonia's smile was sunny.

'We can ask nanny for advice.'

Jack shook his head.

'I don't come from the sort of world where people have nannies! Antonia, I can't give you a big house, a fine car, parties.'

She turned her face towards him, looking like a flower as she stood before him in the sunlight, and he suddenly realised that she was vulnerable, too. He watched her eyes as she spoke softly.

'I don't need them, Jack, but I do need you.'

At last he admitted the need in his heart and reached for her.

'I love you.'

His voice was barely a whisper, but she heard it above the sound of the sea and the crying of the gulls and he saw a deep happiness in her eyes.

'Well, that's a good start!'

He laughed now and reached out for her hands. She gave him one, and then the other. He held them and then lifted them to his lips and kissed her tanned fingers.

'There's a lot to discuss.'

Antonia's eyes were as happy as a child's.

'And all of it nice!'

He felt his lips lifting in a smile as the conviction flowed over him that together they could build a life that would work.

'I could take up law again.'

Antonia gave a cheerful nod.

'It will set the children a good example, to see daddy going to the office every day. You don't have to do corporate law, you know. I've got a trust fund if you want to study again.'

Jack slipped his arm around her

shoulders, hugging her precious form to him. She snuggled in close and he felt conquering masculine pride because he could hold her like this any time he chose. Optimism surged within him.

'I've always been interested in environmental law,' he said thoughtfully.

He turned her gently and they began strolling down the palm-fringed beach together, Jack matching his long stride to her smaller one.

'Would you like to live in London?' he asked.

Her dark lashes opened, and she looked up at him. The trust and the love in her eyes was humbling when he realised that it was all for him.

'Or Sydney. Wherever you like.'

'I'll take the warm climate then,' Jack announced, looking down at her.

She was so beautiful, like a flame in her red dress, that he had to stop and gather her up in his arms.

'Do you think your family would mind flying over for the wedding?'

There was a laugh in Antonia's voice.

'Is that a proposal?'

He held her tight against his chest, relishing the feeling that the missing piece of his heart was filled at last.

'Of course it is,' he said, laughing.

Then he fell on one knee in the swirling surf, clasping his hands to his chest.

'Antonia Everett-Cox, will you marry me?'

She screamed in delight and spun around in a big circle before answering him, throwing her arms out wide and spinning until her red skirt flew about her in a burst of colour.

'Yes! Yes! Yes!' she cried.

She skipped back towards him and held out her arms.

'Oh, Jack, your lonely days are over.'

And as he joyfully swept her up and lowered his head to kiss her, Jack knew they were always going to be happy together.

THREE TALL TAMARISKS

Christine Briscomb

Joanna Baxter flies from Sydney to run her parents' small farm in the Adelaide Hills while they recover from a road accident. But after crossing swords with Riley Kemp, life is anything but uneventful. Gradually she discovers that Riley's passionate nature and quirky sense of humour are capturing her emotions, but a magical day spent with him on the coast comes to an abrupt end when the elegant Greta intervenes. Did Riley love Greta after all?

SUMMER IN
HANOVER SQUARE

Charlotte Grey

The impoverished Margaret Lambart is suddenly flung into all the glitter of the Season in Regency London. Suspected by her godmother's nephew, the influential Marquis St. George, of being merely a common adventuress, she has, nevertheless, a brilliant success, and attracts the attentions of the young Duke of Oxford. However, when the Marquis discovers that Margaret is far from wanting a husband he finds he has to revise his estimate of her true worth.

CONFLICT OF HEARTS

Gillian Kaye

Somerset, at the end of World War I: Daniel Holley, unhappily married to an ailing wife and father of four grown-up children, is attracted to beautiful schoolteacher Harriet Bray, but he knows his love is hopeless. Daniel's only daughter, Amy, who dreams of becoming a milliner and is caught up in her love for young bank clerk John Tottle, looks on as the drama of Daniel and Harriet's fate and happiness gradually unfolds.

T...N

Whe... lbert
was ...nd, a
repla... the
shap... whose
year... rough
marr... ncide
with ... dier's
woman. Christina's obsessive love
for Alain was not returned. The
handsome hussar married an heiress
and banished the soldier's woman
from his life. But Christina was
unswerving in the pursuit of her
dream and Alain found his resis-
tance weakening . . .